THE SPIDER:
THE RED DEATH RAIN

THE MASTER OF MEN!
SPIDER®

THE RED DEATH RAIN

By Grant Stockbridge

ALTUS PRESS • 2019

PUBLISHING HISTORY

"The Red Death Rain" originally appeared in the December, 1934 (Vol. 4, No. 3) issue
of *The Spider* magazine. Copyright 2019 by Argosy Communications, Inc. All rights
reserved.

CHAPTER 1
NIGHT OF DOOM

TWO MEN ducked around the corner from Deacon Street into the darkness of Lancey and bowed their derbies into the wind that whimpered up from the river. Their overcoat collars were about their ears and their heels rang crisply, hurriedly, through the bitter December twilight. Before a lighted shop-window rimmed with frost, they paused, huddling together.

"This must be it," one gasped. He dodged to the door and went in quickly, the other man crowding his heels. They stamped their feet and made blowing noises and the door shut hard after them. In a dark doorway across the street, Richard Wentworth blew out a long breath that made frosty funnels from his nostrils and kicked his heels against the stone step. He was frowning heavily. It looked as if the Commissioner of Police—his personal friend and public enemy—had been right in his estimate of the anonymous note predicting a crime, "terrible enough to interest even the Spider," in Steve's Tobacco Shop across the street. The Commissioner, Stanley Kirkpatrick, had dubbed it a crank note. Wentworth had thought it worth investigating—even if, as he half suspected—it were only to learn that some over-ambitious member of the underworld was seeking to lead the Spider into a trap....

He had been waiting in this doorway for an hour, freezing

In all sections of the city, hundreds fell
dead from the mysterious epidemic....

his feet and ears in vain. So far no murder car had whizzed around the corner to mow him down. Nothing suspicious had occurred in the shop. There was no movement at all in the street, no sound save the thin cold wail of the wind and the squeaking of the swaying sign in front of Steve's shop, where those two men had entered.

Around the same corner from which they had dodged shiver-

ing into the wind, another man came slowly. His coat collar was down, his head up and he moved with a stiff arrogance, swinging a cane in a lightly gloved hand. As Wentworth watched the man, his eyes tightened and he stood absolutely still. Something about that tall thin figure made him strangely alert—made alarm bells sound in his brain. Yet the man had done nothing.

Wentworth jerked his head impatiently. He was being a

damned fool. Just because a man chose to walk upright instead of leaning into the wind, just because he ignored the cold of the December waterfront… but he knew that wasn't the cause of his sudden tension. Somehow that thin, almost skeleton-like figure, with its head perched upon a scrawny neck like some ugly bird's seemed… seemed *evil*.

Wentworth moved his broad shoulders in an irritated shrug. The long wait had got on his nerves. His mind flew back to Kirkpatrick. There had been a gleam in Kirkpatrick's eye when he had shown that note to Wentworth, when he and Nita Van Sloan, his fiancée, had dropped in at the Commissioner's apartment for cocktails.

"We have looked into this casually," Kirkpatrick said. "We found nothing, but it is barely possible that the great amateur criminologist, Richard Wentworth, might care to look into the matter."

Wentworth had laughed lightly at the dig, then he had read the note:

> "On Tuesday night, Steve's Tobacco Shop on Lancey Street will be the scene of a crime terrible enough to interest even the Spider."

That was all, but it had been addressed personally to Kirkpatrick, and now he passed it over to his friend, whom he knew—for all that he had never been able to prove it—that Richard Wentworth was the mysterious nemesis of criminals who called himself the Spider. There was a queer, sharp challenge in Kirkpatrick's gray eyes.

WENTWORTH KNEW the Commissioner intimately. Through their duels as Spider and Commissioner, they had developed an enormous mutual respect. And he knew now that Kirkpatrick was asking him to investigate this thing, more, was daring him into it. Nita's keen eyes had detected the challenge also and it puzzled them both.

His seeking for an explanation, his bewilderment came back to him now as, half angry with himself, he watched this emaciated man stalk with his peculiar half-mechanical stride that was so strangely like that of an animated skeleton. Before Steve's Tobacco Shop, the man paused, slowly turned his head. It was more than ever the evil likeness of a bird, that slow pivoting head upon the scrawny neck. Wentworth crowded back against the wall and caught his breath. He had a fleeting impression that the man's eyes had looked directly into his! For a time that seemed minutes long, the man stared; then, he turned with the same deliberation that marked all his movements and entered the shop.

Wentworth stared indecisively at the frost-rimmed window which effectually concealed everything within the shop. He hesitated to enter. Actually, nothing had occurred to arouse his suspicions, nothing but the tenseness that had swept over him at sight of that skeleton man. Abruptly he stiffened, turning his head to listen. A cry like the wail of a suffering child keened through the cold air, muffled and half-strangled. The sound sent a curious tremor over his nerves. It was repeated twice more. Wentworth took two swift strides toward the curb and checked, staring.

The door of the shop across the way opened once more and the wailing rose to a crescendo. A cat burst from the place and scampered squawling across the street. It ran as a cat does when a bullet has smacked into its ribs, twisting and writhing in the midst of every bound, tail lashing.

Wentworth's eyes jerked from the vanishing cat to the shop. The door was shut again, and against its opaque yellow glass was outlined the gaunt squared shoulders and head of the thin man. He stood just outside, drawing on gloves. Wentworth's breath was coming fast between clenched teeth. His mind was whirling with wild conjecture. But nothing had happened, nothing to stir him like this. A man had walked down the street and entered a shop. A cat had squawled and fled, deserting the warmth it loved for the bitter cold of the night. But what of it? Only taut nerves had made him read into ordinary things an evil and meaning that was not there. Thus he counseled himself.

He stood tensely watching while the skeleton man, as Wentworth had christened him in his mind, turned deliberately and paced toward the river. In a moment the cold black shadows had swallowed him. All that was left was the echo of the slow, regular tapping of his cane. A frown of indecision creased Wentworth's forehead. Should he follow the man or continue his apparently useless watch over this shop? He jerked his head impatiently. It was not like the Spider to be swayed by intangibles, to allow a mere feeling of suspense and evil so to disturb him. Yet he could not put it aside. He felt death in the cold whine of the wind. He could *smell* it.

Wentworth threw back his head to laugh at himself, and in that position, with his mouth open, he froze with horror.

ABRUPTLY, WITHOUT warning, hoarse and fearful screams burst out within that shop across the street. And this time there was no doubt that the screams were human! They were terrible. They shrieked of incredible agony, as if human flesh had found a voice in the instant of dissolution!

With long, bounding strides, Wentworth plunged across Lancey Street. Even as his hand closed on the handle of the shop's door, it was snatched from his fingers. A man staggered out. His arms waved rigidly. His head was wrenched back between his shoulders and his legs lifted cumbersomely in frantic strides. And as he ran, those hoarse terrible screams tore from his throat.

Wentworth whirled from his path, his back to that lighted window, and stared, blood pumping hard through his temples. The man took two, three, four fumbling strides toward the gutter. Suddenly, he bent double. Black blood poured from his mouth. He pitched face down on the pavement. Shuddering convulsions rippled over him; then his body stiffened.

With a wrench, Wentworth tore his eyes from the dead man. But he did not stare into the store. He peered into the cold shadows toward the river, the shadows that had swallowed the skeleton man. It was an instinctive action. For perhaps two seconds, he gazed into the blackness, then he cursed, flung himself into the tobacco shop.

On the floor, another man lay face down in a pool of blood that spelled death. Behind the counter a white-faced boy stared with fight-crazed eyes. He held a nickel-plated revolver in his hand. He lifted it and began shooting.

"Stop it, you damned fool!" Wentworth howled.

He flung himself to the protection of the counter. He heard the window crash to the floor under the pelting of bullets, heard the revolver hammer begin to click on empty chambers. He sprang up, sprawled across the counter, wrenched the gun from the boy's hands.

"You crazy fool!" Wentworth said again, but his voice was cool and quiet now.

The boy stared at him for a moment with the wide eyes of a sleep walker. Then he buried his face on his arms on the counter and his shoulders shook with sobs. Wentworth's eyes narrowed. Those shoulders were wide and competent as a football player's; the face, despite its whiteness, had a determined chin, an intelligent forehead. He did not seem the type to lose his head thus in an emergency, yet he had opened wild fire at the first glimpse of a man coming through the door.

The youth's behavior was not the only mad thing to occur. Nothing seemed sane about the entire night's happenings. In heaven's name, what had killed those two men so horribly? Why had it been done? More than that, why had it been desired that the Spider be on the scene? Wentworth's mind was whirling with unanswerable questions. The boy's sudden shots had even startled the Spider into forgetting his disguise, the character that he had assumed to watch the shop. He stared at the shop attendant's quivering shoulders.

"Wot's the matter, mytey?" he asked and, leaning across the counter, shook him with an impatient hand.

Already noises of alarm filled the street—shouts and excited responses. Within moments, the police sirens would shrill through the night. Wentworth repeated his query and the youth raised his head. His shoulders still quivered with sobs, but there was no tracery of tears upon his cheeks. He stared without comprehension with his eyes still like a sleep-walker's. Wentworth's gaze narrowed. There was something damned strange about this business. This man might or might not hold the key to the problem, but... He slapped the clerk on the cheek, once, twice, three times.

A shudder rippled over the youth's body; his shoulder muscles jerked. His eyes seemed to focus for the first time. For a full minute he stared at Wentworth's face; then he thrust a stiff arm forward, jabbing a finger almost into Wentworth's eyes.

"You did it!" he said sharply. "You did it!"

"WENTWORTH STRAIGHTENED slowly," frowning. Madness piled on madness. He had never laid eyes on this youth before, yet apparently was recognized by him. Not only that, but he was accusing him plainly of these horrible deaths! It was insane, but it was a fact. Wentworth had dressed in character with the neighborhood, and he was not a prepossessing figure in his present disguise. That didn't make it any easier for turn to face this broad-shouldered youth and his accusation. It would not help when the police came either. Wentworth's splendidly developed six feet of manhood was diminished by drooped shoulders, by a rusty old sweater that sagged below his hips. A shapeless greasy cap was low over his brows.

"Are you balmy?" he demanded of the tobacco clerk. "You never saw me in your life, you didn't, until I ran in here after them toffs screamed. Now, look here. You get yourself in hand, mytey, so's when the bobbies come you can tell them a straight yarn. Wot happened in here?"

"You killed those men," the boy snapped. He put a hand on the counter and vaulted easily over it. He seemed suddenly larger, full of bounding youthful energy like a substitute romping onto a football field. He seized Wentworth's shoulder.

"You came in here earlier tonight, and… and…." The exuberant sureness of his voice faltered. He frowned, and his hand dropped from Wentworth's shoulder. He passed the hand to his forehead, heavily, as if he were abruptly weary.

Heel taps in the doorway jerked Wentworth's head that way. A girl stared white-faced at the death upon the floor, then turned and ran to the boy. She caught hold of his coat lapels.

"What happened, Stevie?" she cried.

Steve shook his head heavily. Wentworth looked them over swiftly. The girl had dragged a coat on over house pajamas. Her head, golden hair streaming about her shoulders, was bare. The cold had bitten red splotches on her cheeks. She was small, even slight. Her small white hands clung to Steve's lapels. "Please, Stevie, what happened?" she asked again.

Wentworth moved softly toward the door. Sirens were wailing in the distant darkness now. A scrambled crowd of men and women stared morbidly at the corpse in the street and forgot even to shiver in the cold wind. Up toward Deacon Street, heavy feet slapped the pavement, running; a policeman approaching.

Wentworth's thoughts were whirling with the fearful import of these deaths, with the crazily contradictory things that had happened. There were no wounds upon the victim's bodies. There had been no one to strike them down, yet they were horribly dead. What had done this? What was the reason behind these murders? There was no answer to those questions, but one thing was sure. The Spider had deliberately been led to the scene. And that meant another criminal had arisen who felt himself powerful enough to challenge the Spider. Yet most criminals avoided the Spider as if he were death himself—as he often was for them!

SUDDENLY, TERRIBLY, a man screamed outside. On the heels of that sound, a woman's shriek of pain and terror tore the night. Among those in the morbid crowd that stared down at the body on the pavement, a man and woman seemed to go abruptly mad. Good God! Had the killer struck again? Wentworth stared with his heart pounding high in his throat. The woman tore at her throat. Her clawing, fingers caught the neck of her dress and ripped it and she kept on clawing, digging fingernails into the flesh of her throat and breasts. Her head wrenched back between her shoulders and she collapsed with a gush of blood from her mouth.

The man was running in circles, screaming into the night. Then he, too, pitched to the pavement. The crowd scattered with shrill cries of fright. The policeman who had been running from Deacon Street pounded up and stood puffing, eyes flaring wide

11

as he stared. He gulped audibly. Wind tugged at the clothing of the dead, flapping it with a small cracking noise. There was no other movement.

Wentworth felt horror and anger gnaw at his soul. There might have been some motive for those other killings but these were senseless, without purpose. In heaven's name, what new terror threatened the people of the city, heralded by these hoarse, dying screams?

He moved slowly forward until he stood beside the policeman, staring down at the dead. The faces of the two lying there were terribly contorted. They were no longer human. They were the faces of animals that had suffered unendurably. The policeman jerked his shoulders, bent over. People were coming back from the shadows now, but they still kept a wary, fearful distance from the corpses.

Abruptly, Wentworth stiffened. From the corner, another woman screamed, but not this time with the fingers of death gripping at her throat. It was a voice Wentworth recognized: the voice of Nita van Sloan, the woman he loved!

"Dick!" she cried. "Danger! Kirkpatrick! The Skeleton Man!… Ah-h-h!"

Her scream broke off in a smothered cry as if a palm had been clapped over her mouth.

"Dick!" her voice ripped out again. "They've got me, but…."

Then silence—a hideous pregnant silence….

CHAPTER 2
BETRAYED!

AT THE first cry, Wentworth had sprung into action, racing toward the spot from which Nita screamed. He heard the policeman curse, heard heavy feet beat the pavement in his wake. Wentworth raced on, lips squeezed into a grim line. What in heaven's name was Nita doing in this forsaken neighborhood? What had made her scream? She had come to warn him, that much her scream made clear. She had been seized almost within reach of him. By whom? And what did that cry about Kirkpatrick mean?

These thoughts were a flash in Wentworth's brain as he sprinted toward the spot where Nita's voice had sounded. He gripped an automatic in his right hand and his eyes pierced the blackness ahead. On the corner, the wind spun a street light in erratic circles and its white spot of brilliance moved like something solid and sharp-edged across the humped cobbles.

"Coming, Nita!" Wentworth shouted as he ran. He reached the corner of Deacon Street and paused, staring swiftly right and left. Gaunt tenements and warehouses reared black in either direction. At distant corners, other street lights executed their weird wind dance. That was all. Save for gesturing shadows, there was no movement in the street. Yet here, a moment before, Nita had screamed "They've got me...."

In the six or seven seconds it had taken him to race to the corner, Nita and her assailants had vanished!

Wentworth cursed raggedly, spun about as the cop pounded up and stood panting out white puffs of frozen breath. "What the hell?" the officer gasped.

"A woman screamed," Wentworth snapped. Then remembering his disguise, "But she ain't in sight now. Gorblimey, maybe she was kidnapped!"

The cop peered at him from beneath the visor of his uniform cap, his hand wrapped around the butt of his revolver. "We'll take a look together," the policeman decided, breathing hard. "You know that woman what screamed, mister. I heard you yell to her."

Wentworth's jaw tightened, but there was no time for argument. Every second lessened his chances of finding Nita, of rescuing her from whatever danger threatened. What in God's name had she meant by that cry of Kirkpatrick and the Skeleton Man! Good Lord! The Skeleton Man! Could that mean the gaunt evil man who had strolled into the shop just before death had struck?

"Ow Kaye," Wentworth acquiesced, "but it won't do no harm to hurry, it won't."

He raced up Deacon with the cop pounding behind him. A block ahead, a police car skittered sideways into the street with a screech of its siren and a low whine of hot rubber. The green light on top showed it to be a lieutenant's car. It bored toward them. Brakes squealed and it slewed to the left of the street, not ten feet ahead.

Wentworth ran toward it. A man out of uniform, running

with a gun in his hand, would be an invitation to get shot in the back.

"Around the corner," the cop gasped at the men in the car. "Four people murdered. We heard a woman scream up here. This guy," he turned and looked belligerently at Wentworth, "recognized her voice and called her name."

THE LIEUTENANT stared narrow-eyed across his driver at Wentworth. "Bring him back!" he ordered shortly.

"Listen, lieutenant," Wentworth began a protest, but the tightening of the man's lips told him it would do no good. A break for it then? Not with three guns ready to blaze, and a street of blank, un-lighted walls blocking any chance of escape. Rage burned hotly within him—urged that he attempt it. He forced himself to calmness. It would be impossible to hunt Nita and her assailants with police hot on his heels. Already it was too late to hope to overtake them. Obviously they had access to some one of these buildings. By this time they could have slipped through to another street and driven away.

Wentworth's shoulders sagged. He shuffled his feet "Ow kaye, lieutenant," he mumbled in a thick Cockney whine.

He turned, shambled back the way he had come, shoulders hunched high about his ears.

"Hold on," the cop drawled. "I'll take that gun."

Wentworth surrendered it without quibble. He had a permit for it under the name of the character he had assumed, Snuffer Dan Tewkes. He told the policeman so as they tramped heavily back along Deacon, leaned shivering into the whimpering wind of Lancey Street. Two more police cars had rocketed into the dim stretch by the river now. The hoarser wail of an ambulance siren was approaching.

Policemen moved with loud heel noises around the bodies on the pavement, the circles of their flashlights jerking over them. Their voices came clearly in the crisp cold, their words seemingly visible in steam-like spurts of breath. They looked up sharply as Wentworth and the policeman approached. The cop laboriously told the lieutenant what he knew, which wasn't much.

The lieutenant was a short man with a small man's cockiness. He had a thin, small mouth and hard round eyes. He jerked out little nods like periods to the cop's sentences. When the police-man came to the part about Wentworth shouting Nita's name, the lieutenant jerked his head toward him. The small mouth tightened; the round eyes got harder.

"Inside," he snapped. "I want a good look at you."

"I hain't done nawthin', Lieutenant," Wentworth whined, moving toward the door of the shop with cringing shoulders.

The man called Steve was answering a policeman's questions with quiet words, frowning with an obvious effort at exact accuracy. He looked more than ever like a college boy with his wavy brown hair and the squared manliness of his shoulders.

"These two men said they were going to meet a friend here," Steve was saying slowly. "They bought cigars, three for a quarter Dutch Masters, and lighted up. Then, in a few minutes, one started walking around in a circle, sort of funny like. Then they began to scream…" He choked off, rubbed a hand across his high white forehead.

The girl had wrapped both hands around the bicep of his

left arm and was hanging on. She looked at Wentworth and her blue eyes went wide. She jerked at Steve's arm! "There he is!" she whispered.

Steve pulled up his head. His nostrils quivered once and he nodded quickly so that the front lock of his wavy brown hair sprawled across his forehead.

"That's the man!" he said excitedly, jabbed his finger in Wentworth's direction. "He came in about an hour ago and said he was waiting for two men. I caught him tampering with the cigar case and ordered him out. Then he came running in after those two men started screaming."

WENTWORTH STARED at the boy with a frown. Was he crazy or was this a deliberate lie? He had never been in the shop until the moment when the screams had brought him plunging across the street. Yet there was a queer sincerity in the boy's words. Damn it, the boy meant it! He actually believed what he was saying.

"Look here, Lieutenant," Wentworth protested in his cockney whine, snuffling through his apparently malformed nose.

"This guy is balmy. I never laid eyes on him or 'is bloomin' shop, I didn't, until I hears these toffs screech and comes runnin' across to see wot's up. This guy is standin' behind the counter with a gun in his 'and, and he blayzes away at me, he does. He looked like he was full of dope, he did. Just you awsk 'im abaout the tall, thin toff what comes in here before these men started screechin'. Awsk him wot made 'is cat squawk and run out of 'ere like hell fire was behind it."

Steve was frowning. "No thin man came in here," he said

finally. "And my cat didn't make any noise at all. That stall won't get you anywhere."

Wentworth stared at him calculatingly. Was the boy deliberately lying? He could see no evidence of it and the Spider was a keen reader of human faces. What then was the meaning of his denial?

A frown made vertical creases between Wentworth's eyes. He felt a chill coursing through his body. Once more, he was sure, he had stumbled upon the beginning of fearful crime—upon the initial act of some new and horrible criminal undertaking. The man who wielded the death that had laid these men low could become a fearful menace. Especially if he could enter a shop and spread that death without the men involved being aware of his presence!

Wentworth's tension grew. As if these threats were not enough, he knew that coil after coil of entangling circumstance was being looped about him. Without even showing himself, without revealing his motive, the master criminal was reaching out to smash the Spider! Wentworth turned to the police. He could see from the sneer of the lieutenant's tight mouth that his words were wasted. His appearance was certainly against him, with that greasy cap and the Cockney whine. There was nothing for it except to make a getaway. He would have to discard the disguise and identity of Snuffer Dan permanently, for the gun the policeman had taken from him would reveal his false name and residence.

These thoughts whirled through Wentworth's mind even as he talked, even as he swept a covert glance over the grouping of officers outside the door. His mind was in a turmoil. The world seemed to have gone mad. Men died screaming and there was nothing to indicate how they died; Nita screamed and vanished; this boy accused him of complicity and apparently believed what he said—and there was that Skeleton Man....

But Kirkpatrick was Wentworth's warm friend. The Police Commissioner long had fought him as the Spider, sometimes narrowly missing success. Ultimately, he had become convinced that Wentworth was the Spider, but he had no proof of it. Besides, he entertained a wholesome admiration for the Spider's achievements. Striking outside the law, usually in defiance of it, the Spider exacted vengeance, wiped out criminal threats to the populace that Kirkpatrick could not touch.

So Kirkpatrick had declared an armed truce. So long as proof was lacking, he would assist Wentworth in his battle. If the definite proof ever proved, that Wentworth, wealthy scion of the state's earliest settlers, was that mysterious killer of the night, the Spider, he would strike with the full power of his office against his friend. For the law, despite the fact that the Spider's kills were aimed at wiping out criminals, could not condone his actions. It could not consider motives. He killed, so the greatest benefactor the modern world had known was, in legal eyes as a mere murderer.

No, Wentworth could not believe that Kirkpatrick was involved in any way in this situation. As for the Skeleton Man. THE CLANGING of a heavy door jerked Wentworth's thoughts back to his present situation. At the curb stood a lithe sedan and the man of whom Wentworth had been thinking,

Stanley Kirkpatrick, Commissioner of Police, was striding from it. His saturnine face was set as he entered the shop, punctiliously returning every salute of his men. He stopped in the doorway, a dull red from the cold coloring his high cheekbones. Wentworth started as the Police Commissioner's eyes met his. There was something strange in their steely glance, something hostile and menacing.

"That man is in disguise, Lieutenant" Kirkpatrick's clipped voice stated. He indicated Wentworth with a nod of his head. "Strip it off him."

The lieutenant stared closely at Wentworth, glanced to the keen face of his chief. Kirkpatrick was calmly brushing his spike-end mustaches with gloved fingers, his eyes burning into those of his friend. The lieutenant stepped close, jerked off Wentworth's cap, stripped off the stubby blond wig, the putty-built nose. Kirkpatrick allowed a thin smile to crease his cheeks.

"Richard Wentworth," he said softly. "I suspected as much."

Wentworth smiled easily, took a short step forward. "Yes, Kirk," he said. "I was down here investigating that tip of yours about this tobacco shop and walked in on a murder."

Kirkpatrick's tight-lipped smile did not change. His eyes continued hostile. "I gave you no tip, Wentworth," he said coldly. "Don't attempt to wriggle out of this. I have positive proof that you plotted and committed these murders!"

Wentworth gasped. He stopped in his advance and stared fixedly into Kirkpatrick's eyes. There was raw hatred there! His mind flashed back to Nita's cry. *Kirkpatrick* and *The Skeleton Man!*

What in heaven's name could it all mean? "Handcuff him!" Kirkpatrick snapped. "Put leg irons on him, too. He's a dangerous criminal and we can take no chances whatever with him."

CHAPTER 3
BEHIND THE BARS

THERE WERE four cops and Kirkpatrick between Wentworth and the door. In front of the counter stood the lieutenant and Steve with the girl still swinging on to his arm. Her blue eyes were wider than ever and he could see the tautness of her body where the pajamas pulled tight over her thighs and breasts. Her lips were blue with the cold that came in through the open door and smashed window, but she didn't seem to know it.

Wentworth shook his head slowly. He stood damned little chance of crashing out of this trap. Suddenly he wasn't sure he wanted to get away. He was certain that the nub of the mystery rested on Kirkpatrick. It had been Kirkpatrick's tip that had sent him down here in the first place. And now a queer hostile light blazed in the eyes of the Police Commissioner who usually was so friendly. It was damnably puzzling.

"I want a little private talk with you, Kirk," Wentworth said quietly. "I wish you'd put out an alarm for Nita, too. I heard her scream up the street here just after the last two murders. She said 'They've got me.' I think she was kidnapped, though we were on the spot within seconds and couldn't find any trace of anyone."

He spoke calmly, but impatience burned within him, impa-

21

RICHARD WENTWORTH

tience and fear. He knew that he was face to face with strange and hostile powers, with an agency that killed horribly without appearing on the scene, without inflicting an apparent wound. And Nita, dear Nita, was in the hands of these powers! Furthermore, it could no longer be doubted that the powers had laid an elaborate trap for Wentworth—a trap in which his dearest friend, Kirkpatrick, conspired to hold him!

Kirkpatrick was snapping rapid inquiries at the police while they put on the manacles. He ordered a broadcast of Nita's description. To Wentworth's repeated request for a private talk, he waved an impatient hand.

"There'll be ample time for that," he said, "in jail! But don't think that you'll wriggle out of this. You were caught red-handed this time."

"That's asinine," Wentworth snapped. He started once more to tell what had happened, but choked it off. There was no use. He knew that Kirkpatrick would not believe. There was something completely mystifying about this situation. It was inconceivable that Kirkpatrick had deliberately sent him here to be caught—that Steve's testimony accusing him could have been framed in advance. Hell, even granting all these cold-blooded preparations, they could not have foreseen what disguise he would assume, and it was necessary to know that to have Steve prepared to identify him.

Wentworth jerked his head about sharply to stare at a policeman who was making queer sounds in his throat. The man reeled away from the counter. In his hand was a cigar he had mooched from the case. It was lighted and perhaps a half inch had burned. As Wentworth watched, the cigar fell and with a clawing gesture

that was by now horribly familiar, the officer began to tear at the neck of his overcoat Hoarse screams bubbled up in his throat.

"See, Kirk!" Wentworth barked. "Now blame *that* death on me!"

The man was not dead, but even as the words fell from Wentworth's lips, the policeman's lips shrank back horribly from his teeth and blood squeezed out. He pitched through the broken window, swung there caught on jagged ends of glass while he screamed out his life.

"It's the cigars," Wentworth snapped. *"The cigars, Kirk!"*

With his manacled hands he pointed at the lighted cigar that the policeman had been smoking. It lay upon the floor within a thin line of gray smoke eddying from its charred end.

KIRKPATRICK EYED Wentworth steadily. "Thanks," he said, "you saved us a lot of trouble. That's tantamount to a confession."

Angry words surged to Wentworth's lips, but he choked them down. Argument could win him nothing. He felt a rising tide of despair like the weakness of a grave body-wound flood over him. Kirkpatrick could not or would not accept anything that was in his favor. And whatever power had arranged these deaths was still striking like a blind panther among the men present. Some fearful poison must be in the cigars. He recalled swiftly that Steve had said the first two to die had smoked them. But in the street a woman had died. She would not have smoked a cigar. The poison must be in cigarettes also!

Kirkpatrick seized upon the same idea. He ordered the tobacco cases sealed, ordered tests of the tobaccos and examination of the corpses. Steve Jardin was standing rigidly, arms clasped about the girl whose face was hidden now on his chest.

"Jardin," Kirkpatrick addressed the boy. "You'll have to come along with me. We don't need the girl. Get her name and address."

She gave them haltingly. Delia Hardesty was her name, and Kirkpatrick prepared to depart. Wentworth became aware of the creeping bitterness of the cold. He was lightly clad, in keeping with the poverty-stricken role he played, and his resistance had been lowered by that long watch from the sheltered doorway. He felt the quiver of his muscles. A policeman took him by either arm, shoved him out into the frosty night, into a patrol wagon.

At headquarters, Wentworth's demand that he be ushered immediately into Kirkpatrick's presence was flatly refused. He persisted and the jail keeper slashed at him viciously with a length of rubber hose. After that, Wentworth sat tensely on his steel-framed bed and waited in silence. His hands were knotted in white fists upon his knees. His mind felt numb from ceaseless and futile canvassing of the happenings of the night. It was like the scattered and scrambled pieces of a jig-saw puzzle of which no two pieces seemed to fit together. Nita's abduction seemed totally without reason. The blind, wanton murder at the tobacco shop was equally without motive. It seemed definite; too, that Kirkpatrick had conspired to place him in this predicament. Certainly, he had lied about giving him the anonymous note about Steve's Tobacco Shop.

Suddenly Wentworth started to his feet. Nita had disappeared because she had seen Kirkpatrick give him that note!

Was Kirkpatrick her abductor? But that was ridiculous. Slowly, the Spider sank back upon his hard cot. If Kirkpatrick were responsible—if he were behind these crimes or connected with them—he would pay as all criminals paid to the Spider soon or late. If anything happened to Nita… Something like a hard sob thrust up into Wentworth's throat, but it made no sound. His lips set in a grim straight line. He was like that when, four hours later, four police came to his cell, handcuffed him again and escorted him into Kirkpatrick's presence.

WENTWORTH'S FIRST thought was that they had found out something about Nita, but his eager glance to Kirkpatrick, his quick question, met only a slow shake of the head.

"There has been no word of her," Kirkpatrick growled. "She left her apartment a little before nine and hasn't returned." There was a grim tension about Kirkpatrick, too; drawn lines were carved on his saturnine face. Behind him, the window showed a high line of frost rime, on which street lights glittered coldly, but no more coldly than his eyes.

"Wentworth," he said, "there is no use in beating about the bush. We have you dead to rights. There have been thirty more of these deaths such as…."

"Good Lord, no!" It was a cry that hurt Wentworth's throat with its vehemence. Thirty more were dead! It was even as he had suspected from the happening in Steve Jardin's shop. Some fiendish murder plot was under way. For his own dark purposes, a killer had loosed this new and fearful death upon the people of the city. The inexorable syllables of Kirkpatrick's voice jerked him back to his own peril from the nightmare of horror that raced through his brain.

"We've got you dead to rights, Wentworth," Kirkpatrick was saying. "Steve Jardin says you were tampering with his cigar case an hour before the first of the murders. The men came in, smoked those cigars and died. In every other case when we have been able to trace back the purchase of the tobacco involved in these thirty other deaths, the tobacco shop clerks remember having seen you there in your Cockney disguise. It's an open and shut case, but why did you kill them?"

Wentworth stared fixedly into Kirkpatrick's gray gaze and once more its stark hatred chilled and puzzled him. It drove from his mind the mounting murder toll, focused his attention on the fact that unless he could escape from the police, he would be totally unable to battle the killers, to ferret out the hellish purpose back of the wholesale murders.

"Don't be ridiculous," he said harshly to Kirkpatrick. "That shop of Steve Jardin's was the only one I've entered today. And you know why I went there. I don't know why you choose to deny it now, but you showed me a note hinting at these murders in Steve Jardin's shop. You know that investigation of crime is a hobby of mine. I went down to look over the place and the murders occurred while I was keeping watch."

"I suppose," Kirkpatrick was sneering, "that you were just investigating when you tampered with the cigar case?"

Wentworth took a step forward and rested his manacled fists on the edge of Kirkpatrick's desk. He ignored the policeman's guns, jerked level to cover him.

"I never entered that shop before the men screamed," he said flatly.

Kirkpatrick's small smile was irritating. He lifted his hand to his mustache, parted it with thumb and forefinger.

"In the face of Jardin's story," he said, "that is ridiculous."

WENTWORTH LAUGHED shortly. "Had it occurred to you that Jardin might have something to cover up?" he demanded harshly. "That he might be the one who poisoned the cigars?"

"Jardin has a witness to your presence," Kirkpatrick said shortly. "He is the son of a very prominent family here in town, working his own way because he loves Delia Hardesty. The family lawyer, Dewitt Ahearn, called to see him this evening just as you were leaving. Delia saw you also."

Wentworth frowned heavily, shaking his head. Damn it, such a perfect frame-up could not exist. It wasn't possible, and yet here was the evidence piling up against him and here was Kirkpatrick, smirking with hate in his eyes. Still he could not blame anyone for accepting Jardin's story. The boy's words bore the stamp of truth.

"It's a frame-up," Wentworth snapped. "Can anybody swear that the lawyer was there?"

Kirkpatrick nodded. "The cop on the beat saw him. He's a tall man, thin as a skeleton, and you couldn't...."

"Like a skeleton!" Wentworth's words were a cry. "I saw a man like that enter the shop a second before the men screamed."

Kirkpatrick slammed to his feet, his palm crashing down

on the desk. "Take him away," he barked. "I've heard enough of his lies."

"Kirk, for God's sake!" Wentworth beat his manacled hands on the desk. "Is everyone crazy? You know I'm not lying. I tell you, this skeleton man…."

Rough hands yanked him backward toward the door. Wentworth whirled, striking out with his handcuffs. He caught a cop back of the ear, sent him reeling. With a smothered cry, Wentworth seized the man's gun wrist, wrenched, snatched the weapon free. He whirled.

"Hands up!" he cried. "All of you. I…."

A blow caught him on the side of the head and he reeled. He spun toward the door, snatched at the jamb and whirled around it, firing two shots into the floor. He heard Kirkpatrick snapping orders, heard an uproar break out in the halls beyond, the clanging of an alarm bell. He caught up a chair and hurled it through a broad-paned window, then crouched behind a typewriter desk.

The policeman whose gun he had seized held the keys to these handcuffs. He was in Kirkpatrick's office now, nursing his head where Wentworth's manacles had struck. A queer tight smile crossed Wentworth's lips. There was not one chance in ten that he could get those keys, free his hands from the cuffs and escape from this building, but he had become convinced in his brief talk with Kirkpatrick that no peaceful power could free him from the cell. And he must be free. He must find and free Nita, crush this demoniac criminal who was killing by scores, and he could find Nita only by conquering this man. He had no other clue.

29

What this Master Killer intended—why his death struck so haphazardly—Wentworth had no means of knowing. But the attack upon himself, upon Nita, had not been haphazard. Every cog had fallen exactly into place in the machinery intended to railroad him to prison, perhaps to death. Even his trusted friend....

He saw Kirkpatrick plunge through the door of his office with a long-barreled revolver ready in his hand, two policemen at his heels. A glance at the smashed window and Kirkpatrick whirled toward the hall door.

"Don't waste time staring out there," he snapped as a policeman ran toward the window. "Wentworth wouldn't do anything so obvious as that. Cover the door, block the hall, then search the building."

WENTWORTH SMILED twistedly. If Kirkpatrick had been slow to recognize any clue that might point away from him, his brain had lost none of the keenness that had harried the Spider through many a close race. But Wentworth had not hoped to fool anyone by that trick into thinking he had left the building. He saw the policeman with the handcuff keys, re-armed now, take up a wary stand by the door, his eyes scanning the office alertly. Wentworth remained perfectly quiet until the sounds of the chase had faded down the hall, then he drew his manacled hands back over his head and tossed his gun through the open door of Kirkpatrick's office.

The rattle of its fall jerked the policeman's eyes that way. He got up on his toes, started creeping cautiously toward the sound. Wentworth waited until he was almost in the office doorway, his back turned, then crossed to him with long silent strides. He struck again with the manacled wrists and the officer crumpled without a sound.

It was the work of moments to unlock his handcuffs, snap them about the policeman's wrists. He thumped the officer again carefully with the man's own blackjack and stretched him just inside the hall doorway. Then Wentworth took Kirkpatrick's chair, sat behind Kirkpatrick's desk—and waited.

There was a frown upon his forehead,—a frown of absolute bewilderment. Slowly he removed the last traces of the make-up so that his hair became crisp and black above a lean tanned face; his gray-blue eyes were piercing and his mouth was square-set and firm. In the arch of smooth black brows was a hint of mockery. The slouch was gone from his shoulders and even as he sat behind the desk, the self-confident poise of the man, his vital strength was evident. This was Richard Wentworth—this was that nemesis of evil-doers, the Spider.

Within five minutes, he heard a commotion at the door which marked the discovery of the handcuffed policeman, heard Kirkpatrick's voice raised briefly in sharp anger, then footsteps approached steadily. Kirkpatrick stepped into the office. His eyes were on the floor, his lips pursed. He closed the door, moved toward his desk, then glanced up into Wentworth's eyes. He took the step he was making as if what he saw was slow to register in his brain. Then he halted, rigid in every muscle, and his gray eyes narrowed slowly.

"Have a seat, Kirk" said Wentworth softly.

He reached forward, twitched up the light on the desk so

31

that the full dazzling beam struck Kirkpatrick's eyes. A spasm of anger quivered across the Police Commissioner's face and the hatred that had writhed like a snake in the depths of his eyes was there again.

"Sit down, Kirk," Wentworth ordered again and his voice had sharpened.

Kirkpatrick's right hand jerked at his side. With the precision of slow-timed machinery, it moved upward across his coat toward his lapel. There was a gun there, Wentworth knew, not the long-barreled police revolver, but a compact and deadly automatic. Kirkpatrick was making no effort at a speedy draw. He was simply lifting his hand with slow and deadly persistence.

Wentworth circled the desk in a stride, slapped Kirkpatrick with the blackjack. His friend reeled under the blow. He shook his head in a dazed way, then crumpled to the floor, joint by joint. Wentworth stood staring down at him and the palms of his hands were wet. A chill prickled along the back of his neck. His friend had meant to kill him in cold blood though he had sat there without a weapon in his hand!

A SHUDDER shook Wentworth. He crossed swiftly to the door and peered out. The outer office was deserted. Swiftly, Wentworth took Kirkpatrick's black overcoat and derby from its rack and donned them. He took up Kirkpatrick's cane and, using glue and a pair of scissors from the desk, made himself a neat little spiked mustache like the Police Commissioner's, out of Kirk's own hair. He would pass through no brightly lighted place in leaving the building. This would suffice—this and Wentworth's sure imitation of Kirkpatrick's stalking manner of walking and stiff-necked, military bearing. This was not what he had intended, this sneaking escape from police headquarters. He had wanted to talk to Kirkpatrick, to ferret out the reason behind the hatred. Now that was obviously futile.

He strode from the building without hindrance. He had left too many times with Kirkpatrick not to know what route he followed, what orders he gave, where his car was parked. He had the uniformed chauffeur drive him to his own apartment, dismissed him for the night. Then he made several stops at cigar stores and bought a supply for tests.

He was certain his apartment would be under surveillance. Probably his telephone wires had been tapped, but he must communicate with Ram Singh and arrange to remain in hiding. Still in the sketchy disguise of Kirkpatrick, Wentworth stalked into his apartment building. Police guards were there. A uniformed officer stepped from a darkened doorway, reported with a salute that no one had entered. Wentworth nodded briskly.

"Who's watching upstairs?" he asked shortly.

"No one, sir," the officer stammered. "Orders from headquarters were to...."

Wentworth rasped a curse at the inefficiency of headquarters and stalked to the elevator. While the boy ran the private cage of his apartment upward fifteen floors, Wentworth pondered on this quirk of police hounding. Why had headquarters sent instructions that the guard was to be kept only on the first floor? He shook his head. There was something strange about such orders.

He left the elevator at the door of his penthouse apartment quietly, crossed to the portal in a stride, pressed the bell. He heard it buzz faintly within, but no one came. Wentworth frowned. One of his servants was always at home: Jackson, his chauffeur, Ram Singh, his faithful Hindu body servant; old Jenkyns, the butler, was away on a brief vacation. He shook his head sharply, inserted the key again and thrust the door wide.

"Come out, Wentworth," he called. "It's Kirkpatrick. Hiding will do no good."

Not a sound sifted out from the interior of the many-roomed apartment. Wentworth closed the door, stalked into the living room with the stiff-backed posture of Kirkpatrick. With a sudden scrambling of feet, a man plunged from behind a high, over-stuffed chair.

"You're not Kirkpatrick," the man said, his voice high and flat. "You're Wentworth."

With a start, Wentworth recognized Steve Jardin, spotted a revolver in his hand. The gun was leveled, the boy's finger tightening on the trigger.

"You stole Delia from me!" the boy shrilled. "Now die!"

And in his white, twisted face, Wentworth read death....

CHAPTER 4
THE DRAGON'S CLAW

WENTWORTH LIFTED his hand slowly to his derby. He snapped it from his head, hooked it neatly over the muzzle of the boy's revolver. Steve Jardin started backward, staring at the hat and Wentworth was on him. The boy was as powerful as the build of his shoulders indicated, but *jiu-jitsu* takes account of strength. The pistol came free in Wentworth's hand. He had to punch Steve twice before the fight was over and he stood staring down at the boy's unconscious form.

Wentworth slipped out of the overcoat, tossed it to a chair and stood with his fists on his hips. There were two strange things about this attack. Steve Jardin had been under arrest as a material witness less than an hour ago, and Delia Hardesty, his fiancée, had been, apparently safe in her home. But now Jardin had slipped past police guards and had lain in wait for him in his apartment—to charge him with complicity in the girl's disappearance, evidently—and the police had not even been on watch on this floor! Good Lord! Had Kirkpatrick gone so far in his hatred that he had arranged for this youth to enter and ambush him? Wentworth could not believe it, and yet, what other explanation was there of his presence here, inside the police lines?

Steve Jardin moaned, tossed his big body on the floor. Wentworth thoughtfully dropped the captured revolver into his coat pocket. Another thought struck him sharply, sent him striding through the apartment. Where were his servants? He failed to find any trace of them, but neither could he discover signs of violence. He returned swiftly to the room where the boy lay. Steve was sitting up now, with his head in his hands. At Wentworth's entrance, he reeled uncertainly to his feet, shoulders rolled forward aggressively.

"All right, let's have it," Wentworth snapped at him. "Why

did you come here to waylay me? How did you get out of jail and how did you get in here?"

"I told you why," Steve growled tightly, his lips close against his teeth. "You stole Delia because she was a witness against you. And, by God, you'll either bring her back or I'll kill you!"

There was a slightly hysterical edge to his voice; He stood very straight, with his hands clenched at his side, his head thrown back in a half-theatrical defiance. But Steve Jardin was sincere enough. As before, Wentworth was convinced that the boy believed what he said.

"My fiancée was kidnapped tonight also," Wentworth said quietly. "Kidnapped while you and Delia were standing in your shop. You heard her scream. I tell you this so that you may see that there are other forces at work besides myself. I had nothing to do with Delia's disappearance."

The boy's belligerence became slightly uncertain.

"Don't you realize that you committed first degree burglary when you entered here with a gun?" Wentworth demanded. "How did you get in here? How did you get my servants out?"

The boy's dark steady eyes studied Wentworth warily, the quiet smile on firm lips, the commanding gaze of the blue-gray eyes. It was a vital, powerful face, a countenance to inspire confidence, to command—the face of the master of men. The boy's eyes wavered.

"It wasn't burglary," he said stubbornly. "The servants were out when I got here. I just opened the door and walked in.

"You just…" Wentworth felt muscles tighten in his shoulders, in the calves of his legs. Here was more evidence of this damnable conspiracy which was being aimed at him. Someone had made sure that Steve could enter the apartment and lie in wait for him.

With a curse, Wentworth whirled in a quick, close scrutiny of the room. He had been through his apartment searching for the servants, but he had not been looking for ambush. Item by item, Wentworth scrutinized everything in the room. Nothing was out of place, nothing missing. Abruptly, his eyes centered on the wide French doors that opened on the terrace. Was he mistaken, or had the light shifted on a moving figure there?

HIS HAND dropped into the pocket where he had thrust Steve's revolver. He was thinking swiftly. A shot was risky business, with the police on watch below, but he was up fifteen stories and this was an expensive building. The walls were thick and sound insulated. Furthermore, there were no other apartment spires near. His was the only tall building. He would have to risk it.

"Steve," he said swiftly, lips motionless. "When I shoot, throw yourself to the floor."

The boy's eyes flew wide; tenseness crept into his poise. Wentworth's hand snapped from his pocket and the bullet smashed out the ceiling light. Darkness dropped upon the room and the moonlight on the terrace shone coldly through the windows— shone and outlined three figures crouched against the French doors!

Wentworth's revolver pivoted toward the doors, then a hoarse cry rose in his throat. One of those three figures was gaunt and tall, like a human skeleton in man's clothing. Even as Wentworth stared—as his gun hand came up to fire—the man swerved from view. The other two figures remained stationary against the glass. One of those wore a turban on his head and Wentworth raced toward the doors with his heart cold within him, with a stabbing suspicion in his mind....

He slapped open the French doors, hurled himself to the right, prone upon the icy roof. Cold gravel bit into his hands like fire, and a spear-point of powder blossomed in the darkness from the black mass of a dumbwaiter shaft. Lead splatted against the brick wall behind him. Wentworth's gun slammed twice in answer and two death-screams pierced the night. He rolled, peered up at those two nearby figures motionless against the glass. He gasped a curse. His suspicion had been right. One of those motionless men was his Hindu servant, Ram Singh; the other was the sturdy Jackson. That damnable skeleton man had plotted to have Wentworth kill his own men!

With a curse jagged in his throat, Wentworth poured more lead into the shadows. The tall figure was not in sight, but bullets sang through the crisp cold of the night. A scream answered Wentworth's third shot and he hurled to his feet, sprinting forward in a dodging charge. He hurled his last shot at a spurt of orange-red fire, saw a man rear to his feet and stagger backward against the roof rampart, then sink down limply.

In two strides, Wentworth reached his side, snatched up an automatic that lay beside him. His own revolver was empty and there might be more of these killers about. He crouched, listening. Wind whined thinly about the building. Feet grated on the gravel and Wentworth whirled toward his apartment, gun hand raised. He checked just in time. Steve Jardin was sprinting toward him.

"Stop right there," barked Wentworth.

Steve slowed up, but kept on walking. "I still don't understand, sir," he said, and there was deference in his voice. "But I can see you were telling the truth. You are being attacked, too."

"Stay there," Wentworth ordered. He made a swift circuit of the roof. There was no sound save his own grating feet and the far-off murmur of traffic. He hoped desperately that it had drowned any noise of shots that might have reached the street level. It was possible. Sound tends to rise, rather than descend. HE FOUND the dumbwaiter shaft head torn open, found the two bodies of men he had slain when he crashed onto the terrace. With Jardin's willing help, he dragged the two men who had fallen before his guns to the doors, then stepped quickly to Ram Singh's side. The Hindu was unconscious, his turbaned head sagging limply on his neck. He had been bound hand and foot, lashed upright against the door. Jackson was similarly secured. Wentworth dragged the two inside hurriedly. He found himself trembling with cold as he strode to his outer door, listened for some sign that the shots had been heard. He knew that the apartment just below his was vacant, and he had the entire top of the building to himself.

Finally satisfied that no alarm had been given, he went back to Ram Singh and Jackson, discovered they had been drugged. He found the hypodermic pricks in their arms, but so far as he could determine they were in no immediate danger. He covered them warmly, then turned to Steve Jardin. He studied the youth's face, and this time Steve's eyes met his directly. There was pain in them.

"I'm half crazy, sir, over Delia's disappearance," he said. "You say that your fiancée has been kidnapped, too. I've made up my mind that if you'll help me find Delia, I'll help you."

Wentworth continued to study him. He was not entirely convinced of the youth's sincerity. Steve might have recognized that for the present he could do nothing to harm Wentworth and think that he might do better by appearing friendly. Nevertheless, Steve Jardin could give him some valuable information.

"Tell me how you happen to be free when you were being held as a material witness," Wentworth urged. "And how did Delia disappear?"

Steve drew a heavy hand across his white high forehead, nodded once. "After you escaped from police headquarters," he said slowly, "the report of the chemist came in. He could find no poison in the cigars and the toxicologist reported that all those who had died were apparently victims of heart disease, super-induced by too much smoking. He couldn't reconcile the bloody vomit with that finding."

Wentworth's exclamation of surprise interrupted the story. "No poison!"

Steve shook his head. "They couldn't find any trace of any either in the cigars or in the bodies. Said all of those who died were heavy smokers—that this fact undoubtedly had contributed to their deaths."

Wentworth took an abrupt turn up and down the room, smacking his fist into the palm of his hand. "That's impossible," he said sharply. "The poison must be there. They simply failed to find it."

Steve Jardin stared at him but said nothing. Wentworth stopped before him once more, nodded for him to proceed.

"They turned me loose after that," Steve said. "I went to see Delia and she had disappeared. Her room was turned upside down, everything spilled in the middle of the floor. She put up a fight for it. I thought of you…" He broke off. "It was natural. I was sure you were—guilty and Delia could confirm the fact that you came into the shop that other time…."

"I didn't," Wentworth denied flatly. "Did someone actually come into your shop dressed as I was?"

Jardin was staring at him wide-eyed. "But you did, sir. You were there. I wouldn't lie about a thing like that."

Wentworth stared at him curiously. "Was this before or after your family lawyer called?"

The boy's muscles jerked in a mild start of surprise. "Why, after," he said slowly. "What difference does that make?"

"I don't know," said Wentworth slowly, "but there's a tall thin man mixed up with this thing somewhere. A thin man that makes you think of a walking skeleton." He recalled, with a rising slow tension in his breast, the aura of evil that had seemed to waft from that man on the dark cold street. He shook his head sharply.

"Presently," he said, "I'd like you to take me to the home of your family lawyer. Would you mind staying here with my servants for a few moments?"

HE STRODE, frowning, down the hall. Events had moved

so swiftly since he had been back in his apartment that there had been little opportunity to worry about police pursuit, but he realized it was only a matter of time before Kirkpatrick found how he had escaped from the headquarters and checked up on the apartment guard. Wentworth knew he had been fortunate in that he had left before a shift of desk officers was due to go home. It was possible that Kirkpatrick had not recovered consciousness until too late to question them. Still, he would have to abandon this disguise as Kirkpatrick and slip from the building as quickly as possible.

He strode out through the French doors to the two men who had fallen prey to his gun and dragged them into the apartment. The men were Chinese, and neither was the skeleton man!

Wentworth searched their clothing hurriedly, but there was no clue whatever to their identity. Even factory labels and laundry marks had been removed. Only one thing was common to them both. On the right forearm of each was a small disc-like burn. Under a magnifying glass, this showed as a brand, a brand shaped like the five-clawed feet of the Imperial Dragon!

A slight smile twisted Wentworth's mouth. He slipped a platinum cigarette lighter from his vest pocket, touched its base to the five-clawed brand on each slain assassin's arm. When he removed the lighter, a spot of crimson glowed where the burn had been, a bloodlike spot with hairy legs and poised venomous fangs, *the seal of the Spider!*

Deliberately, then, he picked up the bodies one at a time and hurled them over the terrace ramparts into the darkness of the night, to plunge to the nearly deserted street fifteen stories below. With Steve Jardin beside him, Wentworth went rapidly to the servants' elevator and descended, carrying with him a small black satchel.

At the bottom of the shaft, he waited with the door closed. He heard the hoarse siren of an ambulance in the street, then slipped furtively out into the basement. As he had expected, the alarm of those two bodies plunging into the street had drawn police guards from the hall and he had little trouble in slipping out, merging with a crowd which apparently had sprung from the sidewalks to gather morbidly about the corpses.

Apparently, no one had yet discovered the Spider seal upon the men's arms for he heard no comment about it. He kept a close watch on Steve Jardin but the boy made no effort to signal police or betray the man he had promised to help. A few minutes later, Wentworth got a taxi and drove away. There was a grim smile on his lips. The Skeleton Man would soon have his message through the newspapers, the Spider's seal blotting out his own five-clawed dragon brand!

CHAPTER 5
TRAILED BY DEATH!

WENTWORTH FELT a hard satisfaction in the kills—in the message of the Spider to the Skeleton Man. It was good to find that he was fighting actual men now, rather than the phantoms they had seemed to be before. Death had struck down the first of the victims nearly twelve hours, before; Nita had been kidnapped, his servants drugged. Yet so far his only contact with hostile forces had been this boy, Steve Jardin—until his bullets had found billets in the bodies of those Chinese.

His satisfaction was short-lived. Once more the harrowing thought of Nita in the hands of these insensate killers, as she must be, and the mystery of Kirkpatrick's hatred, returned to harass him. The knowledge that the murders might go on unhindered for all he could accomplish made his blood run cold. He slumped lower in the seat, coat collar up about his neck. A sign on the taxi window read *"heated,"* but the frosty breath drifted from his nostrils-with each exhalation. The driver, bundled in a short, heavy jacket and huddled down behind his wheel, kept the windows tightly closed.

Wentworth impassively held out his cab near the apartment building where the lawyer, Dewitt Ahearn, had his quarters while Jardin entered to ascertain if the man were at home. Jardin had his story all set: He was to ask help in locating Delia; when he left, Wentworth would enter secretly and confront Ahearn. There were some questions the Spider wished to ask. Jardin might give the alarm, but if he did Wentworth could easily escape in the cab. It was a good time to test Steve's fidelity.

The taxi driver slid back the glass that shut off his section from the back of the cab, turned a red-nosed face that peered out between pulled-down hat and high coat collar.

"Say, mister, you gotta smoke?" he asked huskily. "I been dying for one, but ain't had the nerve to get out of the cab in this cold."

Wentworth impassively held out his case of cigarettes, tucked one between his own lips. The driver lighted up while Wentworth fumbled for his lighter.

"Must be way below zero," the driver mumbled, "but you got to keep going to keep living these days." He blew out a cloud of mingled smoke and frosted breath, followed by another. Wentworth found his lighter, snapped it into flame, but, with it half-lifted to his smoke, he paused, staring at the driver. A chill raced down his spine. The man's eyes were staring wildly. Some invisible force was lifting his chin, wrenching his head back between his shoulder blades. A hoarse scream tore from the man's throat and Wentworth almost echoed the cry.

With another screech, the driver wrenched open the door, reeled to the sidewalk, his legs flung high in a sort of fantastic goose step. But he was moving aimlessly, without direction. Wentworth cursed, slammed out of the cab, darted toward the man. Another hoarse scream ripped out, then he doubled forward and pitched to the pavement in a final convulsive wrench of death.

WENTWORTH STOOD staring down at the life shuddering from the man's body, then he looked at the gloved hands. One still grasped the glowing butt of the cigarette Wentworth had given him. Wentworth felt his throat go tight and he glanced at the cigarette between his own fingers. There was no doubt about it. *His cigarette had killed this man!*

With a curse, he stooped, snatched the burning butt from the dead driver's fingers. He heard a squeal of brakes, looked up swiftly to see a night-hawk cab spin to the curb.

"Get a cop!" Wentworth bawled at him.

Footsteps rasped on the pavement and Jardin uttered a low amazed oath at his elbow. Wentworth whirled to him as the second cab spurted away.

"Give me your cigarettes," he snapped.

Dumbly, Jardin yielded a crumpled package.

"Now get to my apartment and destroy all the tobacco in the place," Wentworth ordered. "It's poisoned. This man borrowed a cigarette from me and it killed him. In some way, those fiends managed to put poison in them…."

He broke off suddenly, realizing that the cigarettes had not been out of his possession since before the first of the victims of this strange death had fallen. That meant the cigarettes had been *poisoned while he carried them!* He shook his head sharply. It wasn't possible that anyone could have got close enough to him to substitute poisoned for his regular smokes. With hands that were rock steady, he opened his case and examined the contents closely. No, these were his own special blend of cigarettes.

But there was no tune to stand here seeking to fathom the secret of the poison. Police would be here at any moment. This new death would add more damning evidence to the false testimony that already condemned him.

"Ahearn at home?" he snapped at Jardin.

The boy, still staring down at the stiffening body of the cab driver, shook his head. "He's at Deacon Coslin's place." He gave a Park Avenue address. "Been there all night."

"All right. Get back to my apartment. The police will probably come there soon, but for God's sake, destroy the tobacco before it kills some one else." Wentworth crossed the walk in a bound, sprang to the seat of the dead man's taxi, and sent it hurtling around a corner. He flung back a single glance as the line of buildings cut off his view. Jardin was moving away fast, his head wrenched about to stare at the body on the pavement.

WENTWORTH MADE one stop on his way to Deacon Coslin's place. He mailed all the cigarettes he carried, including the stub that had brought death to the taxi driver, to a trusted friend, Professor Brownlee, for analysis. He jotted a brief note telling that the city chemists had failed to find poison, but that he was sure the cigarettes carried death. Then he raced on. Traffic lights were out and only an occasional car with a huddled driver muttered along the double-laned avenue of New York's Gold Coast.

There was a cold sweat upon Wentworth's forehead as he crouched over the wheel. He wiped it away with the back of a gloved hand. It was not that he had escaped death by the chance of a man bumming a cigarette. He was used to death, used to risk and hair-line escapes. It was the sinister and deadly persistence with which the persecution of the Skeleton Man followed him. He had seen that gaunt, evil outline only twice now and each time, men had died horribly. It was maddening to see the murderer's victims fall about him and to be helpless to avert their doom. It was terrifying that so far he had been able to form no idea of the purpose behind these kills.

And Nita! Unless Kirkpatrick was behind it—which Wentworth still could not believe—why in the name of heaven had she been kidnapped? Before this, she had fallen into the hands of fiendish killers, but always she had been seized with the intention of forcing Wentworth to drop the battle. Surely no such action was necessary yet. He had not even found a single reliable trail—had struck only at two underlings. Furthermore, if Nita was to be held hostage for his noninterference in the battle, why had not her captors communicated with him?

He shook his head in sudden weariness, dragged his hand against his forehead. This trail he followed was dim at best. It was foolish to suspect a respectable family lawyer of such crimes as these, merely because he was thin and tall. Wentworth stopped the cab three blocks from the address Jardin had given for Deacon Coslin, stepped briskly to the street, and took his satchel from the tonneau. The cold made him gasp. He bowed his head and pushed into the wind.

Deacon Coslin. The name was abruptly familiar to Wentworth. The man was the head of a religious cult founded by himself. As Wentworth concentrated on the name, fragments of information began to drift back into his memory. Wentworth received voluminous clippings on every conceivable subject from newspapers and magazines, and it was his custom to study them energetically for hours every day when the pressure of his ceaseless battles with crime would permit.

He cursed softly as he recalled suddenly when last he had seen the name of Deacon Coslin. The man—who, had merely arrogated the title "deacon" to himself—had declared war on smoking. He and his congregation had prayed for the judgment of the Lord upon the "sinners who smoke."

This was ridiculous, Wentworth told himself. A fake priest of a fanatic cult—a cult which, however, had drawn many purse-heavy women to fill its coffers—had prayed for judgment on the smokers of the nation, and men and women died with cigarettes and cigars in their mouths! And now the trail of the Skeleton Man, supposing Dewitt Ahearn could be so called, led to his establishment!

Palace would be a better name for Coslin's abode, Wentworth amended. Pictures of it had been spread in Sunday newspaper supplements, pictures of the great black Negroes who, turbaned and naked above the waist, were the servitors of the place. Apparently fanaticism, supposing it was accompanied by a sufficient amount of surface flourish and hokum, paid good dividends to its high priest.

WENTWORTH HAD reached the corner of Coslin's place now. A stone wall was capped by a spiked iron fence which surrounded an entire city block. Elaborate gardens were within—the place had been erected as a home by a wartime millionaire—and the building itself was a large sprawling thing of marble and iron grillwork and intricate carving. Wentworth pushed on along the wall, head into the wind, watching out of the corner of his eyes. The high, spiked iron gates were closed, and here in front, the street lights coated the pavements, splashed the shrubbery within with silvery brilliance.

The side street, however, was only dimly lighted and great patches of black shadow lay against the base of the wall. He tossed his satchel over, and with a brief run and a leap, Wentworth seized the top of the stone work with gloved hands. He muscled himself straight up until he could get a knee on the top.

It was the work of moments then to hand-vault the irons spikes and drop on soundless feet into the shelter of shrubbery below.

For long minutes after he reached the comparative shelter of the shadows, Wentworth crouched listening. No sound marred the quiet of the garden. Even the faint, occasional hum of a passing automobile was blocked out by the thick stones of the wall. He might have been on an estate in the far reaches of Long Island for all the sound that penetrated. The towering walls of apartment houses did not exist. There was only black shrubbery crowding close about him with bare skeleton branches, and that glittering white facade that was the palace of Deacon Coslin.

While he crouched, Wentworth's hands worked rapidly. Long practice made mirror and lights unnecessary as he lengthened and sharpened his nose, tautened and sallowed his skin and drew on the lank, black-haired wig that was the disguise of Tito Caliepi, whom all the world knew as the Spider. Black cape and black slouch hat came from the satchel and slowly his broadly competent shoulders wrenched and became distorted until the figure that hid in the black shadows became a monstrous crippled thing—a hunch-back of fearful mien....

His disguise completed, Wentworth slipped swiftly through the darkness toward the frosty whiteness of the house. On the first floor, windows were all tightly closed, but the second story showed a number that were slitted open. The fresh air fetish prevailed even in such frigid temperatures. Carefully, Wentworth made his selection—a closed window in a line of open casements—then his hunched figure merged into the black shadow of a close corner behind one of the many porches.

His hands were busy beneath his coat a moment. Then a thin line snaked upward, looped over a railing. Soundlessly, he drew down the two ends of the cord—it was little more than that, less than the diameter of a pencil, but made of the most powerful silk known to man. The Spider's web it was called, and it tested to the strength of seven hundred pounds! Holding the two ends of the silk line, Wentworth twisted it rapidly about his hands and with its help, scaled swiftly to the porch roof. The moon was near the horizon now and her black shadow fell deeply on the spot where he crouched.

Rapidly, he re-coiled the silken line, thrust it away in the kit he carried always strapped beneath his arm—the kit that carried a few indispensable tools. He spanned the distance to the sill of the closed window, and pressing a small stethoscopic suction disc to the pane, listened for sounds within. There were none. Softly, he eased up the window and dropped inside, stepping quickly to one wall.

Then he stiffened, staring toward the shadows of the far side of the room. "Would you mind closing the window?" a girl's throaty voice asked quietly. "And remain inside, please if you don't mind. Otherwise I shall have to shoot!"

CHAPTER 6
A STRANGE RECEPTION

STANDING TENSELY beside the window, Wentworth laughed softly into the darkness. The laughter was flat and mocking, curiously sinister.

"It *is* chilly," he agreed. He reached out with his left hand, slid the window down.

In that brief moment of hesitation, he had analyzed the situation and made his decision. He had small doubt that he could escape as he had entered if he wished, but he wanted to find out about Deacon Coslin's strangely accurate prayers, and Dewitt Ahearn. True, the girl who had spoken, with an exotic slurring accent in her rich voice, undoubtedly held a gun on him. He shrugged.

"Shall we talk in darkness, *signorina?*" he queried softly, "or shall we have light?"

Immediately a soft light glowed rosily against the far wall and he saw the features of the room. The open door of a bath; another, closed, that undoubtedly gave on the hall. A large four-poster bed, beside which, light glowed on a table. Standing beside the bed, a small gleaming gun in her right hand, was the girl.

Wentworth moved forward with the curious limping gait that his twisted back gave him, washing his hands dryly before him.

"Ah, *signorina,*" he murmured, "if always a light turned on in darkness could reveal such beauty!"

"That's near enough," the girl told him shortly. "Stop there!"

The gun lifted two inches by way of emphasis and Wentworth stopped, peered at her from beneath the shaggy brows that were the Spider's.

The girl was above medium height. The heavy cream silk of her nightgown, which was her only clothing, draped about the rounded maturity of her body like a caress. One sloping shoulder, the color of old ivory, was bare where a shoulder strap had slipped; her black hair formed a cascade across it like poured ink. The light made a shadow between her breasts.

Wentworth's eyes studied her face, found himself meeting a dead black gaze that had neither light nor life in it—dead black eyes beneath delicately arched brows that carried a suspicion of almond slant. Her forehead was high and un-furrowed, her lips slightly smiling. "Ah," she said softly, "the Spider!" Once more Wentworth caught that almost indefinable slurring of syllables, but now that he had seen her face he no longer was puzzled by it. The girl was Oriental, north China probably. There was more than a hint of Imperial Manchu blood in those high olive cheekbones.

Wentworth washed his hands once more, sticking to the thick Italian accent of Tito Caliepi.

"It is charming of you, *signorina*, to recognize an old man."

"Sit down," the girl said. Her gun's muzzle indicated a chair by her lamp table and she sank gracefully to a seat on the side of her bed. The heavy silk molded about her limbs as she crossed them beneath the gown's trailing skirt. Her feet, narrow and white, were bare. The nails were tinted black.

Limping across toward the chair, Wentworth felt beneath his feet the deep softness of silken rugs; saw that the bed sheets were satin. Certainly Deacon Coslin did things with a grand manner. But what was this Chinese girl doing in the house of a cult priest? Who was she that she calmly challenged a man climbing through her bedroom window in the dead of night, that she could recognize with a smile that intruder as the Spider, where many men would have trembled and fled?

She even seated herself for conversation, and the gun in her hand was not alert.

WENTWORTH EASED his twisted back into the chair, smiled into the girl's dead black eyes.

"The introductions are only half complete," he said. "It is only fair that I should know my hostess."

The girl appeared to weigh the words. Wentworth tried to estimate her age and found it difficult. Her skin had the fresh bloom of early youth, but her figure had maturity. She might be twenty-three or four. She might be in the early thirties. Her gesture now, as she drew up the traitorous shoulder strap, clasped her hands gracefully upon her crossed knees, certainly was not that of an immature girl. The gun rested beneath her hands. She was less than ten feet away.

"Wu Ya Che," she said finally, "daughter of Wu Chang, who finds the study of American adult religion amusing." She was looking at Wentworth directly with her dead black eyes. The lids were heavy. "You are not an old man, Spider. Your eyes are not the eyes of an old man. When they look at me, they are not the eyes of an old man."

Wentworth laughed softly. Wu Ya Che. It was Mandarin—Peking—dialect, he knew, though he was not over-familiar with the language. He knew, too, what the name meant. *Wu*, five; *Ya Che*, wild chickens. Truly she was as graceful as a wild fowl, but he sensed danger here. This was no ordinary, woman. She had keen eyes, eyes such as Nita had. A twinge stabbed Wentworth.

Nita was in the power of these fiends he had come here to trace and he sat talking with this girl… But there was valuable information to be gained. Wentworth got slowly to his feet, moved with his hitching twisted pace toward the girl while her black eyes held him.

She made no move to use the pistol, but her head moved slowly as he came toward her, her eyes always upon his. When he sat upon the bed beside her, she turned slightly and lay back upon her silken pillows, her white hands rising into the black cloud of her hair. Her breasts lifted and made little pointed mounds against the silk. The pistol slid across the suave curve of her thighs and settled into the bed sheets. There was a slight enigmatic smile upon her lips. He saw that they were pale.

"No, you are not old," she said softly, "but old enough!"

Wentworth laughed softly. "Old enough to know better," he said. He did not touch her. He looked into her face.

"Ya Che," he said, "I can conceive of no reason why you should help me, but if you would tell me where to find the rooms of Deacon Coslin and Dewitt Ahearn you would earn my undying—" he paused, just long enough, "gratitude."

The curve of the girl's lips grew and the faintest gleam of white showed between them. "I, too, cannot see why I should help you. But Deacon Coslin's rooms are to the right at the end of the hall and those of Dewitt Ahearn adjoin them on the left. I am glad to have your undying… gratitude."

She lay watching him and the lids of her eyes were even heavier. They were like the petals of flowers wrought in old polished ivory. Wentworth allowed his shoulders to sway toward

He sprang forward and slapped
Ahearn with the flat of the automatic.

her slightly, his own eyes heavy-lidded. Then he smiled and
stood looking down at her. He stepped back and swept a bow
that was graceful despite the ugly hump that distorted his back.

He had been on the point of making her a prisoner to prevent an alarm, but he knew suddenly and strangely that it wasn't necessary.

The girl came to her feet with a single movement, as lithe and poised as a cat. She was grave and a sudden harshness rasped into her voice.

"We shall meet again," she said. It was a statement, but whether of threat or promise it was impossible to tell. "You needn't fear that I will give an alarm."

WENTWORTH NODDED. "A thousand thanks," he murmured. He opened the door, stepped out into the dark hall, frowned to feel his heart pounding against his ribs. He lifted his hand unconsciously to his forehead, found that perspiration beaded it. And suddenly, standing there in the darkness, he felt a tightening of the skin behind his ears, felt his muscles bunch in his shoulders as though for battle. He felt a weakness as though he had escaped a great peril. And it was strange that he did not worry over an alarm—that he was so confident the girl would remain quiet.

For a full thirty seconds, he stood there while that strange feeling surged over him. It made him angry. He shook it off and pushed on toward the hall end where the girl had said Deacon Coslin's rooms were. It was strange that Deacon Coslin, who predicted the disaster of the tobacco shop, should have a chamber adjoining that of a thin, tall man.

Once more there were deep-cushioned rugs beneath Wentworth's feet as he stole down the dim hall. The only light came faintly up the stair wall, limned his hunched shadow against gray walls. Then he was crouched in the darkness outside Ahearn's door. He had decided to question the lawyer first. He would be less apt to spread a hysterical alarm and so to prevent the Spider from carrying out his full program.

Softly, Wentworth turned the door knob and tested the lock. It was secure. His hand slid to the tool-kit beneath his arm, abstracted a lock-pick of chrome steel. Two seconds and the bolt snicked back. The door eased open beneath his cautious hand. He peered in, then flung himself violently forward.

A light from the hall revealed two men struggling near the window, one, a thin angular man in a flopping bathrobe and another of whom Wentworth could see only hands. The hands were lean and powerful, and yellow-skinned. The villainously pointed nails identified the man as a Chinese. But even as Wentworth sprang forward, the two figures separated. The Chinese sprang for the open window. Wentworth reached him in a bound. The Chinese whirled, knife flashing. A quick wrench, a moment of flaming fury, and guided by Wentworth's fierce strength the knife jabbed into the vitals of its wielder. The Chinese slumped, gasped out his life. Wentworth straightened slowly, crossed to the door and closed it, switched on a hooded light.

Dewitt Ahearn—Wentworth could hot doubt that the skeleton-like man was he—exhaled a long breath.

"Thanks," he gasped. "Another minute and that Chinese...."

Abruptly, he sprang toward his bed, yanked the pillow aside and snatched an automatic pistol that lay there. Wentworth reached his side in a bound and wrested it from his hand. The lawyer retreated a step, caught the bed with the back of his knees and sat down abruptly.

"What does this mean?" he spluttered. "Are you in league with that yellow devil?"

"What yellow devil?" Wentworth asked quickly.

He held the lawyer's automatic ready in his fist and scanned Ahearn with alert questioning eyes. In pajamas, wrapped in an abbreviated bathrobe which parted to show his bony knees, he scarcely seemed evil, even though his head was thrust forward menacingly on a stringy neck. Impassively, Wentworth studied the face.

DEWITT AHEARN was about fifty years old. His hair was grizzled, cropped close to the scalp, showing a skull as angular as his lanky body. His eyes were crowded close up against bushy gray-black brows, and for the rest, the skin seemed to have shrunken across his face until it was strained almost to breaking over knobby cheekbones and hooked nose. It had even shrunk the flesh from his mouth so that compressed lips were pulled up from long squirrel teeth in a perpetual snarl. Certainly not a pleasant face under any circumstance and now, twisted by anger and uncertainty, it was hideous.

Ahearn thrust his angular body forward, long fingers curled into big-knuckled fists, thin wrists upon his knees.

"Speak up," he commanded harshly. "Are you in league with that yellow devil or not? If you are, I promise you it will go hard with you."

Wentworth permitted a slight smile to stir his lips. He could not be sure this was the skeleton man he had seen in front of Steve Jardin's tobacco shop. He carried his head thrust forward with the same poise of an evil bird of prey, and he was thin enough, but beyond that there was nothing. His challenge had been sharp and sure.

"It was very cleverly done," Wentworth said softly, "but it doesn't fool me. You were giving the China boy orders. When you heard me come in, you pretended to struggle with him to alleviate any suspicion."

Ahearn surged to his feet, his movements as stiff as the unfolding of a jointed carpenter's rule. He raised his big-boned hands above his head in threatening fists.

"You dare… you dare…!" His harsh words stopped for lack of breath. Red spots appeared on his taut, sallow cheeks. Wentworth held the automatic alertly at his side and watched. Ahearn's anger seemed genuine.

"What will you gain when Steve Jardin dies?" Wentworth asked sharply.

For an instant, his words seemed to puzzle the lawyer. He frowned the bushy grayish brows down until they buried his eyes. For the first time he appeared to study Wentworth. He stood with his head thrust forward, his sharp-kneed legs slightly bent, the posture of an unusually tall man who perpetually stoops through doorways.

"Just who are you?" he asked. "And what have you to do with Steve?"

"You haven't answered my question," Wentworth snapped. "What profit will you get from Steve Jardin's death?"

The man's straight lips pulled together over his teeth, shut in a narrow line. There was stubbornness, too, in the set of his head on his narrow shoulders.

"Listen," he said, "I don't know who you are and I don't care. If you're not tied up with these yellow devils who are trying to blackmail me, I thank you for breaking in and killing that Chinese. If you're involved, I'd advise you to surrender that pistol and get out of here before I raise an alarm."

WENTWORTH DID not answer and Ahearn walked firmly on his gangly loose-kneed legs toward a bell-button in the wall.

"Wait," said Wentworth quietly. He took three steps backward; his eyes still on Ahearn's face, and stooped beside the body of the dead Chinese. His left hand went from his vest pocket to the Chinese's forehead and returned. Where he had touched, a vermillion spot sprang to life on the Chinese's forehead—the menacing seal of the Spider.

That Ahearn recognized it showed in his narrowed eyes, in the further lowering of those bushy brows. "Ah," he said, and made no further step toward the bell.

"You see now why I ask about the blackmailing," said Wentworth, straightening.

"I'm not entirely sure," Ahearn replied slowly. "The Spider is a killer. Many say he is a great criminal. Police have fabulous rewards out for him. Yet there have been times when he wiped out evil men who menaced the very life of the nation. In fact, I have seen criminals cringe at the mention of the name. They say honest men have nothing to fear from the Spider. But why do you come to me?"

The lawyer's attitude was still uncompromising. Wentworth could not decide whether the fellow was guilty or not. He knew the man had spent much of his early life in the Orient and his silhouette was certainly that of the Skeleton Man whose only two appearances had been on scenes of death. Furthermore, there had been a Chinese in his room when the Spider had forced an entrance. The struggle, as Wentworth had stated, could easily have been faked. On the other hand, this Chinese did not have the dragon claw upon his forearm. Wentworth shrugged.

"If you will answer some questions," he said calmly, "you may help me avert countless murders and suffering throughout the city, perhaps throughout the nation. Incidentally, you can help Steve Jardin. Police still suspect him in connection with these deaths in his shop, and now his sweetheart has disappeared."

Ahearn continued to stare speculatively. "What do you want to know?" he demanded.

"What is this blackmail business that you mentioned?" Wentworth asked.

Ahearn turned his back, walked to the bed, dropped upon its edge with his big-knuckled hands clasped between his knees. "I received threats stating that unless I paid fifty thousand dollars I would, die as had all these others in Steve's shop," he said slowly. "I was ordered to come to this house and the Chinese came for my answer."

"That's all you know?"

The lawyer nodded his head slowly. "The threat came by telephone, and the man spoke perfect English. I don't know how the Chinese is involved."

Wentworth frowned over this information. Was it possible that the wholesale killings had been intended to force people to pay blackmail? The deaths in Steve Jardin's shop would strike close to Ahearn it was true, but the idea seemed absurd. Furthermore, this Chinese involved in the blackmailing did not wear the dragon-claw brand as had the men he had fought, men obviously connected with the tobacco deaths.

"Do you know anyone," he asked slowly, "who would be sufficiently interested in separating Steve Jardin and his sweetheart to commit several very brutal murders?"

AHEARN ALLOWED his drawn lips to relax in what passed for a smile. His teeth were hideous. "Scarcely," he said drily. "His father threatened to cut him off over the affair, but Franklin Jardin is hardly a murderer. And his threat to cut the boy off is not very serious. In a few years, Steve will come into considerable money independently from an uncle."

Wentworth jerked his head sharply in puzzlement. The blackmailing certainly seemed no adequate reason for the killings. There seemed no personal grudge against Steve Jardin that would justify it. His mouth thinned with resolve. Regardless of what he thought of the blackmail clue, he must follow it down. Right now, that lead pointed to Deacon Coslin, since Ahearn had been ordered to come to his house to meet the Chinese blackmailer. But there was still another point to clear up—the witness who said he had seen Wentworth in Steve's tobacco shop. "There is another thing, Ahearn,"

Wentworth drawled in Tito Cailepi's dialect. "A man named Wentworth is being held in the Jardin shop deaths. Jardin said you saw him there—a man in a cap and long, red sweater, speaking with a Cockney whine. Did you see him?"

"I did," Ahearn confirmed shortly.

Wentworth sucked in a deep breath. Either Ahearn was lying or he was subject to the same malign influence that had caused all these others to identify the Cockney figure as having been in their shops.

"I'll have to tie and gag you," Wentworth informed the lean man. "There are some other calls to make and I don't want you spreading an alarm."

The words were scarcely out of his mouth when Ahearn sprang from his seat on the side of the bed. He leaped, not at Wentworth, but toward the bell button on the wall. Before Wentworth could reach him, he had jabbed the button, raised his voice in loud and angry shouting.

"Help!" he cried. "Help! Police! Burglars!"

He stood against the wall, head thrust forward stubbornly, squirrel teeth showing in a mocking smile.

"I don't like being tied up. Spider," he said in his harsh, biting voice. "Also, it seems to me you knew entirely too much about these killings. I think the police would like to question you."

Wentworth went toward him on light treading feet, the gun ready in his right hand. Ahearn crowded against the wall, fists knotted.

"I'm warning you," he said. "That bell does not merely summon the servants. It throws guards all about this house, brings police and special detectives, floods the yard with lights. Deacon Coslin has too many costly things in his house to take chances with burglars."

As he spoke, brilliant white light blazed in through the

window from outside, dimming electric light. The shouts of men rang through the house. Ahearn began to laugh.

"I'm very much afraid, Spider," he jibed, "that you've been caught at last!"

CHAPTER 7
KILL THE SPIDER!

ALL WENTWORTH'S partially lulled suspicions of Dewitt Ahearn's swelled back, but there was no time now to press his inquiry. He sprang forward, slapped swiftly with the flat of the automatic. Ahearn dodged, but not quickly enough. He sprawled down beside his bed.

Before he hit the floor, Wentworth bounced to the dead Chinese, groped hurriedly over his body. He found no evidence of identity on the man. There was no time to make a closer search. He jerked open the hall door, strode toward that of Deacon Coslin. Abruptly, he slowed his swift pace, made it a casual stroll. He turned from Coslin's door and walked toward the stairs. He had heard a door open. As he reached the head of the steps, he glanced to his right and nodded to an aged Chinese who stood there, hands thrust into the sleeves of a resplendent kimono.

The Chinese returned his salutation with a bow. He was bent and fat, and despite the full skin, his face was corrugated with a thousand wrinkles. From his chin dangled a stringy beard, the five-stranded beard of venerable wisdom.

Wentworth started to descend the stairs, then paused. "Are you Wu Chang?" he asked quietly.

The Chinese bowed. "And how does it happen that you know this unworthy one's name?" he demanded politely.

Wentworth bowed in turn. "But everyone has heard of you—that your wisdom is as great as that of your venerable name!"

At this play upon the meaning of his name—literally five elephants—and the wisdom Chinese attribute to the great beasts, small gleams touched the Chinese's eyes. It might have been amusement. But the man was clever. Wentworth could surmise the keen brain behind those lively young eyes. The Chinese bowed again. "You do this humble one too much honor," he murmured and retired into his room.

As soon as his door closed, Wentworth sped back along the hall to that of Deacon Coslin. His brain was racing with conjecture. He was positive that the Chinese knew he was an interloper. Perhaps his daughter Ya Che had communicated with him. Certainly, too, he had not been deceived by Wentworth's complimentary glibness about his name. Was it possible that this aged Chinese was behind the blackmail plot? The man with Ahearn had been Chinese and the men who had attacked him in his apartment were Chinese, too, wearing upon their arms the symbol of the imperial fire-clawed dragon. His daughter....

Wentworth thrust the thought from him as he entered Coslin's rooms and locked the door behind him. The brilliant white light streaming in through the windows made the luxurious over-furnishings of the room clearly visible. The rugs elsewhere had been soft. These seemed ankle-deep. Cushion-laden

69

davenports stretched to left and right, the one on the right upholstered in long white fur. Wentworth wasted no time on this room, but strode toward where light glowed yellowly beneath a door. This, too, was locked, but his tool kit supplied a means to unfasten it speedily.

As he yanked it open, a woman screamed and Wentworth caught a fleeting glimpse of a pink nude body vanishing through another door. Deacon Coslin—Wentworth recognized the man instantly from pictures—finished tying the cord of a silken dressing gown, faced him with a furious, red countenance.

"What do you mean," he screamed pulpit-style, "by bursting into my private rooms?"

WENTWORTH'S MOUTH was thin and set, his eyes steely. "I am the Spider," he said grimly. "And I've come for you." He sprang toward Coslin and the cultist priest staggered back, big arms windmilling and flapping the draped silken sleeves. He was a robust man with a heavy, florid face which, with his six feet two of height, gave him a commanding appearance. He had an unctuous voice and his hands were padded and fat, the kind of hands that stroke women's arms under the cover of fatherly feeling.

Wentworth's lips drew back from his teeth as he slapped with his automatic. He jarred Coslin's jaw and the man flopped back across his bed, squealing small frightened sounds. Wentworth leaned over him, drew back the gun again.

"Please," Coslin squealed. "Please, don't hit me!"

"You leave him alone," a woman's voice snapped. "Aren't you ashamed of yourself, attacking a priest?"

Wentworth jerked Coslin to his feet, slammed him toward the bathroom door where the woman stood.

She shrank back into the darkness as Coslin reeled up against the wall. Hennaed hair was bunched in close curls about her head. She had draped a huge turkish towel about her like a Roman toga, one arm and shoulder bare. Wentworth recognized her, too—a wealthy woman with more money than sense, and a middle-aged husband who found solace elsewhere.

"Coslin," Wentworth said, tight-mouthed, "you've got a secret way out of your rooms for your women to use. Where is it?"

The man stammered sounds that didn't mean anything. Wentworth pinned him against the wall with a hand gripping his throat, the gun ready in the other. He turned toward the woman and his voice was sharp.

"You tell," he snapped, "or I'll batter his pretty face until you won't know it."

The woman gasped. "It's in here," she wailed. "In here!"

Wentworth pushed Coslin before him into the bathroom; saw the woman plucking at the edge of a full-length mirror. It swung open and she huddled aside.

Wentworth shoved Coslin into a narrow hallway behind the mirror, thrust the woman after him and shut the mirror door. He spilled light from a pocket torch over the two.

"Talk," Wentworth said, "and I'll let you out of here. Otherwise, you can stay here and rot together."

Coslin blubbered words that finally made sense. He hadn't known anything about the tobacco deaths; he finally managed to say, until Dewitt Ahearn had come to him with the report of an extortionist. He didn't know anything but that, so help him God.

In the distance, Wentworth could hear an incredible crescendo of police sirens. "What made you forecast the deaths of tobacco smokers?" he demanded. "How did it happen that your prophecy was fulfilled?"

A curiously ecstatic expression settled itself upon the cultist's florid face. His large blue eyes rolled upward and his fat hands clasped before him. "I had a vision," he said unctuously. "The Lord appeared to me in a dream and said unto me—"

"Cut that hooey!" Wentworth snapped.

"It's true! It's true!" the woman said. "He went into a trance while he—while I—while we were in there tonight. When he came out of it, he said the Lord had told him lots more people—all of them smokers of tobacco—would be killed today."

COSLIN NODDED, his big fat face utterly serious. "I don't understand it myself," he said slowly. "I never had these visions before, but they look like good stuff."

Wentworth glowered at the man. He was a charlatan, a woman-robbing crook with his fool cult, but it was apparent that he was telling the truth.

"All right," Wentworth said. "I believe you. Now get up."

Trembling, Coslin got heavily to his feet, his eyes staring into the white beam of Wentworth's light. Abruptly, that light was drowned out in greater brilliance that came from behind, from the mirror door.

"Come out of that!" a voice snarled.

Wentworth twisted his head about. Men in uniform, police

with guns in their hands, blocked the door. Their flashlights were blinding.

"Cripes!" a man gasped hoarsely. "It's the Spider!"

"Shoot him!" cried a voice that Wentworth knew, the clipped precise voice of his friend, Stanley Kirkpatrick. "Shoot him—and shoot to kill!"

Death stared him in the face from the guns of those grouped police there at the entrance to this narrow hallway, but even so, the Spider could not fire on police. There flashed through his brain the thought that Kirkpatrick had gone mad.

Wentworth flung his hands high above his head. "Don't," he screamed in a woman's voice, his lips unmoving. "Don't shoot! You'll hit me!"

He bellowed in a frightened imitation of Deacon Coslin and instantly the man and woman crouched behind him took up his cries. They had been too dazed to act, but Wentworth's swift action had given them their cue. It did not matter that by their screams they helped the Spider. They thought only of self-preservation.

The police, hearing those frightened cries, stayed their guns. Before they could recover from their astonishment, Wentworth sprang backward, squeezed past Deacon Coslin and his red-headed inamorata, so that they were between him and those threatening guns. In two strides he had reached the other end of the passageway and his groping hands discovered the fastening, flung it wide.

Slamming the door shut, he crossed the room beyond in great strides, hurdled the bed and shoved through a tiled bath to a door on the opposite side. As he had calculated, this second room was the luxurious quarters of the girl, Wu Ya Che. It was deserted and he speedily closed the door behind him, crossed to the window.

The outside of the building was coated with the silvery glare of floodlight focusing on windows and doors, turning the shrub-planted yard about it into a garish thing of black and silver metal. Police moved about in pairs—dozens of them with shotguns and rifles. At stations were men with sub-machine guns cradled against their hips. If police had planned deliberately to lure the Spider into a trap, they could not have contrived a better one. For flanking all this armed watch, was the high wall with its spiked top and this too was bathed in the all-revealing glare.

IN THE hall, in the room next door, police were shouting, heavy feet pounded. Kirkpatrick, Wentworth knew, had discovered that hidden passageway where the Spider had sought shelter. There must have been some tell-tale clue that pointed to it, a piece of clothing caught behind the mirror perhaps, or a wet footprint on the immaculate tiles of the bath floor. With that clever brain working against him what chance did he have to escape? But he must be free to fight this gigantic criminal... and Kirkpatrick too. Much as he fought against the verdict, it seemed Kirkpatrick was hand in glove with the Skeleton Man!

Wentworth flung swift glances about him. It was evident that Ya Che had fled from the room in haste. One of her slippers still reposed by the bed. The covers were dragged out on the floor. A closet stood half open... Wentworth bounded toward it, yanked the door wide. An incredible wealth of delicate clothing hung in brilliant array. Swiftly, he fumbled over the garments, found an embroidered silken kimono. He threw it about him and it dragged the floor. He sprang to a mirror and his hands moved like lightning as he laid out a make-up kit that was part of the compact kit he carried.

From the lank black wig of Tito Caliepi, he made a stringy beard and fastened it to his chin. The beaked nose vanished and collodion on the skin in the outer corners of his eyes began to draw them slant-wise. In swift movements, he lined his face with age wrinkles. A scrap of black silk, ripped from a gown, became a skull cap. It was a flimsy disguise, one that would not stand up for a moment before the assault of brilliant lights or under the keen scrutiny of Commissioner Kirkpatrick, but it might gain him a few seconds with subordinates.

A fist beat heavily on the hall door.

"Open up!" a man shouted. "Open up! It's the police!"

Wentworth bent his head forward in a semblance of the weakness of age, shuffled to the door and clattered out Chinese names, names that were meaningless but which were intoned in the singsong of the Peking dialect. He opened the door and stood blinking, his hands in the sleeves of his kimono.

"Anybody in there?" a suspicious cop demanded.

Wentworth bowed, stepped aside. The policeman plunged in and Wentworth instantly popped out and slammed the door shut. He raced along the hall, and as he ran, he emptied his automatic into the ceiling. Ducking down a back flight of steps, he let out shrill frightened squeals.

A policeman barged into his path, gun shoulder hunched forward.

"What the hell's eatin' you?" he demanded.

"The Spider! The Spider!" Wentworth squeaked. He fluttered a trembling hand toward the steps he had plunged down. The cop reached them in a stride and banged upward. Still squealing with excitement, Wentworth shambled along the hall to the front of the house again. He jabbered frightened sounds which included the word Spider and waved toward the front stairs. Two more cops started upward. Wentworth shuffled hurriedly out onto the porch, saw an armored motorcycle with a side-car parked at the steps. Two policemen standing beside it looked up and frowned as he approached. Wentworth reached them at the same instant an upper window flung open.

"Grab that Chink!" a man bawled. "He's the Spider!"

CHAPTER 8
TALONS OF THE DRAGON

BOTH WENTWORTH'S hands flung out from his sleeves. He struck with both simultaneously; an automatic in each fist, and the two men went down. He was out of his kimono in an instant, clapping a uniform cap on his head. A gun banged from the window, but he was already in motion. The engine of the motorcycle roared, and crouched low behind the bullet-proof screen, he spurted for the gates.

"Shut the gates! Shut the gates!" That would be Kirkpatrick, seeing, as ever, the one thing to do in an emergency.

Motor roaring wide open, Wentworth raced for those iron gates, saw two men in uniform running to close them. He raised his second automatic, sent bullets flying over their heads. One man flinched aside, flung himself prone. The other snatched one half the gate, and started it swinging cumbersomely shut.

The man who had fallen scrambled up, sprang back to his task, but Wentworth was almost atop him. He wrenched at the handle-bars, felt the side-car lift as he skated in a sharp, skidding turn. It slapped the moving edge of the other half of the gate, the motorcycle trembled, teetered on edge. Almost in his face, a pistol blazed. Wentworth flung his weight to the right, felt the motorcycle wrest free of the gate and lurch forward. The side-car's tire hit the ground and he was skating into the street.

A swift glance to right and left showed him there was no escape that way. Police were scattering across the street with leveled guns. A man hurled from a patrol-car with a sub-machine gun in his hands. Straight at the grassy stretch between the two lanes of Park Avenue, Wentworth hurled himself, regardless of the low iron fence that surrounded it.

An instant before the front tire would have touched the fence, Wentworth wrenched the motorcycle about. As it slammed sideways toward the low curbing, he sprang from the saddle, vaulted the fence. Crouching low, he darted across the grass and heard bullets clang and sing against the motorcycle and fence. He hurdled again, sprinted for the lighted doorway of an apartment house.

He had gained seconds in his race, seconds that it would take police to reach the end of the parkway or to climb the fence.

They could not fire with accuracy through the vertical palings, even with a machine gun. Two jumps ahead of police lead, he reached the door of the apartment house, plunged through it. He raced up one flight of stairs, found a window opening onto a back-yard fire escape and went out through it in a single swift motion.

He landed hard upon the concrete with a jar that seemed to shake his jaw-teeth and ran on with stinging feet. The courtyard was narrow, but a black doorway led downward on its far side. A dive into that, a race through dim corridors past an opening that flung out furnace heat and he was up on a side street. Swiftly Wentworth stripped off his coats and flung them into an areaway, snatched off his collar and the venerable Chinese beard. Then he merged with the crowd that jammed the street. It was bitter cold, but there were a half dozen other men such as he, shivering in shirt sleeves while they watched the excitement. Wentworth edged up to one such man.

"Ain't we the damn fools to come out like this," he mumbled, through chattering teeth.

"You said it," the other growled in answer. "Well, I got enough of this."

"Me, too," Wentworth grumbled.

SIDE BY side they turned and trudged along the street. A policeman stopped them, "Where you two mugs goin'?" he demanded.

"Home," the man with Wentworth growled. "Sixty-seven East."

78

"Just came out to see the fun," Wentworth added with a grin. "But the cold ain't worth it"

The cop's mouth was glum. "Ain't it the truth. Get along wit' youse."

Wentworth and the man walked on. The man turned into a doorway with a grunt and a wave of his hand. Wentworth shambled on and turned the next corner, slipped into a basement doorway and found a janitor's torn coat. It didn't keep him warm, but it kept people from staring at him.

No one on the subway gave him a second look, taking him for a bum who had sought the warmth of the cars. Wentworth found an abandoned newspaper. His escape from police headquarters was the lead story in the more sensational papers, coupled with news of the mysterious tobacco death. The total was over fifty now. One paper, he could see from headlines across the aisle, had made a feature of the theft of an ambulance containing the bodies of two men who had fallen from the roof his apartment. So the Skeleton Man had claimed the bodies. He had got the Spider's message directly then.

Wentworth cursed. Couldn't the newspapers see the importance of these killings? Couldn't they guess at the horror which threatened? The city should be up in arms hunting the murderers, staying the bloody hand that might even be preparing to strike. With a feeling of cold fear, Wentworth recalled that the false priest had forecast more of the weird killings for this day.

Curiously, he let his eyes roam over the car, curiously, but with sick dread in his heart. Were some of these men going to be among the next victims? Postmen in their gray uniforms going to their early work; Italians in work clothes, a tin lunch box in their hands; young clerks headed for early openings; a few scrub women heading home, telephone girls going on duty. All swaying and lurching in the close stuffy warmth of the subway, shouting a few broken words of conversation above the roar and rumble of the wheels.

As the train neared the stop where Wentworth would alight to work his way toward his Fifth Avenue apartment where he planned another attempt to revive Ram Singh and Jackson, he felt tension, like a muscular tightening of his heart. It was silly to put any credence in the forecast of that hypocrite, Coslin, but, damn it, his previous prophecy had been fulfilled!

Wentworth cursed as the train trundled into the Astor Place station. Then he stumbled out amid a procession of working men. They climbed the steps with deliberation, lighting pipes and cigarettes in the cover of the kiosk, stepping out with caught breath into the cold blast of the wind. For moments Wentworth stood waiting in the protection. Abruptly, without warning, a hoarse scream rent the morning air.

WENTWORTH PIVOTED, saw a man wheeling in wild, frenzied circles, saw him clawing at a straining throat, then collapse in the street in the bloody tobacco death. Even as he fell, three other men were walking in circles. A girl standing five feet from Wentworth puffed nervously at a cigarette, trembling and staring as those other three died with horrid screams.

Their cries found an echo in her own throat her wide eyes turned to Wentworth in a mad appeal, then she tore at her throat with frenzied hands. Her blouse ripped. With some vague idea of helping her, Wentworth sprang to her side, but she was mad with the grip of the death now. She struck at him with clawed nails, screamed and ran wildly. She stumbled and pitched down the subway stairs and did not stir again.

A new crowd was coming upward from another subway train and they shrank back from the fallen girl. Some stopped to stare at her crumpled body, her dress torn awry. Others hurried past with hasty glances. A traffic policeman was running headlong from a distant corner.

A man stopped at Wentworth's elbow, lifted a match in cupped hands to his cigarette. Wentworth struck the match aside.

"Don't smoke!" he urged hoarsely. "That girl down there smoked and it killed her! These men out here smoked and they're dead!"

The man smirked. "Nertz," he said. "What are you, one dese new preachers?"

"Fool!" Wentworth snapped. "The tobacco is poison!"

"Sure," the man jibed. "That's what they used to say about whiskey."

He struck another match and his eyes hardened. "Lay off now, buddy, or youse is goin' to get smashed."

Other men were coming up the stairs, throwing morbid looks at that pitiful body below. "Don't smoke!" Wentworth shouted. "It's poison. The tobacco has been poisoned."

A few glanced at him curiously, but that was all. Street corner cranks were frequent in the city. Sometimes these men stopped and listened to them, jeering or applauding. Now they had jobs to do. They had no time to listen to a sermon against tobacco. The cop had stopped by one of the bodies, run back to his box to call an ambulance.

Hoarse screams burst out again, made the morning horrible.

"See!" Wentworth pointed a rigid arm toward where the youth he had tried to save screamed in his death agonies. "See, he smoked and he's dying! For God's sake, throw your tobacco away!"

One man got white, threw away a pack of cigarettes, but a bum immediately snatched them up and ran off. The cop was pounding back now. Wentworth saw that the officer's eyes were fixed on him and he slipped down into the subway, cursing. What was the use of warning these fools? They would not heed. Then, damn it, the police should be forced to act! He would risk calling Kirkpatrick. The man was enraged at him, ready to kill on sight. But Kirkpatrick had a keen brain. He would see at once the necessity of stopping the sale of the poisoned tobacco. He could not be in league with the killers.

WENTWORTH TRAVELED two stations more in the subway and went into a telephone-booth where they had a dial instrument from which calls could not be traced. He phoned Kirkpatrick and the call was relayed to the Deacon Coslin's palace temple. Presently the clipped tone of the Police Commissioner came over the wire.

"Kirk," said Wentworth, "this is Dick."

Rasping sounds filled the receiver, curses and vilification. "Wait you fool!" Wentworth snapped. "This has nothing to do with you and me. It is much more important than our quarrel or your capture of me. Men and women are dying on the streets from smoking poisoned tobacco. The only way to save them is to stop all sale of tobacco. You can put that through as an emergency measure. Will you do it?"

Kirkpatrick was silent for a long moment.

"If you want to stop the sale of tobacco, it is to further your own nefarious ends in some way." Kirkpatrick declared finally. "I'll see you in hell before I attempt to stop it!"

"Kirk, for God's sake," Wentworth implored. "What's the matter with you? Can't you see it's the tobacco?"

"I see," Kirkpatrick's cold voice droned, "that you wish the sales stopped. I know that my chemists say there is no poison in the tobacco. You are a mad dog, Wentworth, and I shall make it my duty to run you down and kill you on sight. You are a murderer, a poisoner...."

Wentworth clicked the receiver down on the tirade and scuttled out of the booth. His eyes were cold and hard. What in God's name had got into Kirkpatrick that he had taken this attitude? The man must have suddenly gone crazy! Anyone but a mad man could see that it was the tobacco, regardless of what the police chemists said. It would not be the first time that poisons which defied all analysis had been used by a murderer.

Frantically, he hurried to another telephone-booth some distance from the other, and phoned the newspapers. He identified himself as the Spider, repeated his warning against the tobacco. But whereas previously any message from the Spider had received instant and respectful attention, this time the editor swore at him.

"Kirkpatrick phoned about your plot," the man told him vehemently. "If we can help defeat you by not printing your lies, we'll do it!"

Good Lord! Had all the world gone mad? Or was he himself crazy? Wentworth stood outside the telephone-booth, staring ahead with unseeing eyes. A scream ripped him from his preoccupation. A woman was clinging to the tobacco counter with both hands. A lighted cigarette lay beside her. As Wentworth watched, she slumped, dying, to the floor, and dragged the whole case of tobacco down over her in a crashing blast of breaking glass.

In the name of heaven, was the whole city going to be murdered out of hand? Who was behind these fiendishly brutal kills? What was his motive? With a violent curse, Wentworth flung from the store. By God, he would find the killers! But even in his rage, he realized his own utter helplessness. He had not a single clue....

CHAPTER 9
THE ARMY OF RODENTS

NOT A single clue. The words throbbed into Wentworth's brain like the beating of a trip hammer. Then abruptly, he whirled, stared back through the door. Customers were fleeing from the place in a mad rush. The tobacco clerk staggered out the door, flapped his hands, shouted in a thin excited voice.

Wentworth smiled grimly. He reached the clerk in two long

swift strides. "Where do your tobaccos come from?" he snapped. "What jobber do you buy from?"

The man stared at him, mouth opening and shutting without sound. Wentworth caught him by the shoulder, shook him violently, and repeated his question. The man stammered out the name and Wentworth strode away rapidly. Here at last was something definite he could work on. If only police would check on the victims of the wholesale poisoning, find the source of their tobacco. But it was useless to ask Kirkpatrick to do that and without police cooperation, he could not press the inquiry in that direction. He could investigate the one company named by the clerk, however.

There was no means of telling whether the poison was put in the tobacco before or after manufacture into cigarettes and cigars. But since the deaths seemed to be confined to New York City, he assumed the poisoning was done in the city itself. He got himself fresh clothing, phoned his apartment to find police in charge there, and caught a taxi to the warehouses of the firm the tobacco clerk had named, the J.H. Levinson & Sons Company. He bought copies of all the papers and ran hurriedly through them during the trip in the cab. Screaming black headlines hit his eyes like a blow:

2000 DIE IN MYSTERIOUS EPIDEMIC! HUNDREDS FALL DEAD IN STREETS! SPIDER LINKED TO NEW MURDERS!

Wentworth's lips curled back from his white teeth; his blue gray eyes shown like agate. The Spider was blamed. That was

Kirkpatrick's work. Not only was he failing to assist in catching the real criminals, but he was hampering Wentworth by these constant attacks. The police in his apartment prevented him, for the present, from having the help of his faithful servants, who had recovered by now from the narcotics the Skeleton Man had pumped into their veins. The police had severed connection between him and Steve Jardin, whom he might have used.

Rapidly he scanned the papers, found that, as he had suspected, the deaths were confined to New York City—for the present. Whatever the motives of the mad fiend behind these murders, there was nothing to prevent him from spreading his murderous work over the entire country at any time he desired. In his mind, Wentworth saw the headlines that would shriek at the populace when that occurred. Two thousand dead would become twenty thousand, a million. He skimmed through the inside pages and his eyes widened on an advertisement which was spread over a double page. *Denict cigarettes are safe!*

Reading the announcement, Wentworth's gaze narrowed to a pinpoint, but he told himself it was foolish to think that a cigarette firm would poison ordinary cigarettes to put over its own denicotinized variety. Still he could overlook no bets. He would investigate. He rolled the paper into a tight knot.

BENEATH THE disguise he had assumed, his face was haggard and drawn. His eyes burned with a feverish brightness. The Spider battled for 120 million lives—for the safety of the nation's populace. Resolutely, he clung to that idea. He could not permit himself to think of Nita, spirited away during the first clash of strength with these killers. If, as had occurred before, the criminal kidnapped Nita as a hostage to keep him from the battle, why had not some message come to the Spider? To Wentworth, sitting rigid in his taxi, staring straight ahead over the crumpled newspapers, came the answer: Nita was dead.

He could not drive his mind from the ghastly idea. Somehow, in attempting to seize Nita, they had killed her, so there was no need to communicate with him. He shook his head sharply. No, it could not be that. Perhaps the criminal knew the futility of threats in keeping the Spider from his work. Perhaps he sought to cripple him by harassing his mind with doubts—with uncertainty about his beloved.

A hoarse scream jerked Wentworth from his somber thoughts, pulled his eyes toward the streets through which the taxi was grinding its way. They were wedged in a traffic jam at Herald Square, where Broadway and Sixth Avenue with its noisy elevated train structure formed an X at the junction of Thirty-fourth street. Here the great department stores of the city centered, Macy's with its block-long shopper-jammed building; Saks, with its glittering array of windows. A block away, Gimbels sucked in and breathed out a tide of holiday shoppers.

On street corners, men in red suits and white whiskers rang little bells beside iron pots that swung from tripods. A hundred Santa Clauses solicited alms for the poor. They stood on little wooden platforms to keep their feet off the bitterly cold concrete and shifted from foot to foot, ringing their bells in mittened hands. Beyond them, the wide sidewalks were jammed from curb to store-window with throngs that could only shuffle forward.

Men stood at the doors like traffic policemen, parting the throngs, shepherding them in one door, urging another stream out through another. The windows were gay with tinsel, with elaborate displays of gifts and children's toys. With a shock, Wentworth realized that within four days, it would be Christmas. Christmas, and a wholesale murderer was loose in the city!

Once more the hoarse scream sounded, piercing through the clattering roar of the elevated train, through the squawl and bellow of automobiles jammed hub to hub across the street. There was a swirl in the human river beside the subway entrance at the corner of Macy's. People were pushing away frantically from something that was invisible in their close-pressed ranks. But there was no need to see. Wentworth knew the invisible murderer had struck again.

His taxi lurched forward at the change of the lights while police were fighting their way through the thick mob toward that whirlpool where a man had gone down. Suddenly the air seemed full of screams. They came from a dozen spots among the serried ranks. Good God, the death was striking on all sides! Fully a score were stricken. For a moment their screams rang out clear, they were swallowed in a thicker, heavier roar—the roar of panic.

Women's screams pierced high above the bedlam, children's pathetic cries shrilled into the cold air. The entire crowd had gone mad with fear! Fists were flung high. A pell-mell rush split the packed sidewalk mob. A dozen people stampeded straight out into the street. A trolley car, just picking up speed, slammed on brakes with a high pealing of its bell, but it was too late to save one man who screamed from beneath until its heavy iron wheels crunched out his life.

Wentworth hurled himself from the taxi, wedged immovably between a truck and other automobiles, and leaped to its top. Springing from one car top to another, he made his way swiftly toward the center of the trouble. It was like crossing a river by jumping from rock to rock. Here the waters were fear-maddened people, but a man might die in them very swiftly.

"You're not in danger," Wentworth shouted. "You're not in danger if you don't smoke! Stop smoking! Throw down your cigarettes!"

A few white faces turned up toward him, but they were without sense, without reason. If they saw him, he was only another man like themselves, shouting. A man in a red suit and white beard, one of the alms-soliciting Santa Clauses, was swept along like a bloody chip on a flood of destruction.

WENTWORTH STARED down at him, saw the man striking out viciously with both fists. Then he saw the reason. Two children clung to his coat, whimpering and crying.

Wentworth went down off the cab top like a swimmer diving. The impact of his body struck down two men who would have felled the Santa Claus. With a quick reversal, Wentworth landed on his feet, yanked up the two children, tossed them to the top of the stalled car from which he had leaped. He turned, seized the Santa Claus, boosted him up, too. Then he saw that the man had a cornet thrust through his belt.

"We were singing Christmas carols," the man babbled, "singing—and a woman screamed in my face and died."

Wentworth snaked the cornet from the mail's belt. "You're going to sing again," he roared. "Quiet the kids, and see if you can get them to sing again. We've *got* to! Scores may be killed in this stampede."

He slapped the cornet to his lips, blew a shrill long blast on it. A few heads turned toward him, startled at the strange sound. With no more preliminary than that, he sent the silvery strains of a Christmas hymn rolling over the throng.

The cornet was cheap and brassy, but it was loud. The high walls of the buildings caught the sound and hurled it back, threw it down upon the heads of the crowd:

> *Holy night, silent night,*
> *All is dark, save the light.*

Wentworth sent the slow familiar notes of music blasting out. More heads turned toward him now. Policemen were still pushing their way through the stampeding mass, trying to break it into small portions, to disrupt the mad mob spirit of fear that had gripped it.

> *Yonder where they sweet vigil keep*
> *O'er the Babe who in silent sleep*

Behind Wentworth, the thin quaver of a child's voice rose with the words. A second took it up and a rich churchy tenor joined them. Santa Claus was singing, too. A score of faces were turned toward them now. Two men battling their way savagely through the crowd slowed, their eyes straying upward toward the man who played the cornet, toward two children and a man with funny white whiskers and a red suit who sang a Christmas hymn calmly in the midst of a riot!

> *Rests in heavenly pe-eace—*
> *Re-ests in heavenly peace!*

Instantly, Wentworth started it over again. He tooted out a full line of the music, then jerked the horn from his lips and waved it like a baton. Like a choir leader, he shouted at the people:

"All together now," he yelled. "There's nothing to worry about. Nothing at all. *So long as you don't smoke!* Altogether now, let's sing!"

> *Holy night. Silent night.*

The childish voices and the churchy tenor took up the refrain again. Wentworth stepped aside, shoved them forward, two small children with their cheeks dirt-streaked by tears; a bow-legged thin man in a misfitted Santa Claus suit. They sang strenuously, noisily. Wentworth started the cornet again, stopped to urge the people to sing once more.

A few faltering voices took up the song, women first, then the muttering bass of men and suddenly the whole street was filled with a soaring tremendous volume of music. There never had been such a Christmas carol before, twenty thousand men and women throwing song into the air while Wentworth led with a brassy cornet, while the children and the skinny Santa Claus sang.

All is dark, save the light,
  Yonder where they sweet vigil keep
O'er the Babe....

Men in white, with a stretcher in their hands, were wriggling through the crowd now toward where dead men and women sprawled on the walk. They stared curiously at the singing throng, at the group on top of the auto. They picked up their tragic burdens. Here and there, men or women twisted white, distraught faces about, turned desperately back to sing again as if that alone was their hope of salvation from death.

When the song was over, a great breathless hush fell over the multitude. Wentworth stepped to the edge of the car top and lifted his voice.

"Those who died," he shouted, "died because they smoked poisoned tobacco. If you stop smoking, you won't be in any danger. Spread the word! Tell everyone that death is in the poisoned tobacco."

A STIRRING in the crowd at the corner jerked his head that way. Above the ranks, he saw a man in a derby striding purposefully toward him, eyes glaring across the heads of the mob. Wentworth grinned twistedly. Kirkpatrick, summoned by the disturbance, was on hand.

"Get that man!" Kirkpatrick stormed sharply, his voice cutting through the hush. "He's the Spider!"

Wentworth spun toward the man and the children.

"Sing," he commanded, thrusting the cornet into the man's hand. "Sing, before that fool stampedes them again."

The man gaped at him, jerked his head in a frightened nod

and stammered out the first lines of another Christmas hymn. The children caught it up. The song steadied, soared once more with other voices joining in. Wentworth dropped from the auto top into the thick of the crowd and moved quietly away. Kirkpatrick could not make good time through the close-pressed ranks. He was in too big a hurry.

Wentworth found his taxi and clambered in again. The driver was singing, almost under his breath, singing the song that filled the street with its deep-throated power. The truck ahead lurched into slow motion and the cab driver snapped out of the spell. He slammed into gear, squeezed in ahead of another car that by rights should have traveled behind the truck. The other driver blew his horn angrily, shouted something. The taxi man leaned his head out and jeered, Wentworth smiled tightly. Normality was restored.

For the moment, a horrible panic had been averted. The Spider had prevented stampede from adding to the death toll of the murderers. He might have convinced some that the wise thing to do for the present was to quit tobacco, but it was a trifling victory. He hoped the newspapers would carry a detailed story, would quote what he had shouted. It might do some good. He could not help thinking that if it did, Denict cigarettes would profit.

Meantime there was another battle to be fought. The taxi broke finally through the thickest of the traffic and hurried eastward toward the warehouse where the jobber of at least one pack of poison cigarettes stored his supplies. The congestion of automobiles and taxis gave way to the lumbering of heavy trucks between which the taxi darted like a terrier among elephants.

They turned off a main artery into a narrower, dirtier thoroughfare of humped cobbles. The cab slowed, jounced heavily up and down on its springs. Abruptly the driver slammed on brakes with a curse. Wentworth leaned tensely forward, staring through the windshield. His eyes, sweeping the flanking walls, the dingy street, at first detected nothing unusual. Then he stared down at the cobbles and he, too, cursed in amazement.

Up the street poured a stampede of rats! They were all sizes and colors, dirty gray and brown, some as large as alley cats. They scampered along the gutters, slithered along close to the walls, poured a filthy army across the street, and the air was filled with their rasping squeaks of terror!

CHAPTER 10
TRAIL OF THE RAT

THE CAB driver's stop had been instinctive, the halt of a man who a dozen times a day snubs on brakes to keep from running over dog, or man, or child. Now, savagely, he threw the cab into gear, sent it lurching forward, ploughing through the tide of rats. Wentworth stared narrow-eyed about him for the source of the rush. He was suddenly thinking of a dark street where the cold wind whimpered and a rusty sign squeaked, of a man whose every aspect was evil and a cat that fled with squawling fright. Afterwards, men had died screaming, but it had been the terror of that cat which had heralded it all. Now the street was filled with a river of squeaking rats that fled in terror from—what?

The rodents were pouring from windows and doors of a warehouse; a slithering gray stream erupted from the building on his right as he looked.

"Stop at that warehouse," Wentworth ordered.

The taxi swerved to the curb and, watching with frowning brows, Wentworth waited for the exodus from this particular building to end. He searched the street. Only one other machine was on it, the delivery wagon of a bottled spring water company. The workers were not in sight. He searched the walls. They were blank, with few windows, the warehouse sides opening with great sliding doors which were mostly closed now. What windows there were had been broken long since by the stones of street urchins.

Wentworth looked back to the doorway opposite which, the taxi was parked. The stampede of rats was thinning out. It stopped for a moment; there was another gush, then a single gray patriarch who scampered out last of all. Wentworth got out of the cab, ordered the driver to wait. Overhead, the sky was thick with leaden clouds, and after the cold wind of days, a comparative hushed warmth had returned. As Wentworth stalked toward the warehouse door, a few scattered flakes of snow feathered down into the canyon of the street, dissolved on the pavement.

Wentworth looked up and down the street again, saw that the rats had all taken cover. Then he walked up the warehouse steps and into the office. All the employees were clustered excitedly about a girl who had fainted. A man crossed to a fresh bottle of spring water, set in a holder, wet a handkerchief, returned and bathed the girl's temples. The man looked up and saw Wentworth.

"Just a minute, sir," he said hurriedly. "Those rats... Dorothy fainted."

Wentworth nodded slowly, frowning. The girl stirred, sat up. The man came across to Wentworth, dabbing his forehead with a handkerchief.

"Never saw anything like it," he said, his hand trembling. "Kind of scared me. You know the saying: rats leave a sinking ship. Of course, a warehouse can't sink." The man smiled faintly.

"I'm a federal inspector," Wentworth said, flashing a badge half-concealed in the palm of his hand. It was a courtesy badge of the police department, issued long ago when he and Kirkpatrick were still friends. "I want to look through your warehouse."

"Federal inspector!" The man seemed startled, "but what...?"

"Just routine," Wentworth assured him. "Someone has an idea that tobacco is causing all these deaths and we have to check up to see if any of the supplies are tampered with."

THE MAN frowned, then shrugged. "Of course, you can look," he said. He swung open a gate in the office rail and paused suddenly, jerking his head about the girl who had fainted was screaming, screaming terribly. Wentworth saw that her clenching hand had crushed a cigarette. Her head strained backward; her hands were clawing... Wentworth cursed harshly. The warehouse man sprang toward her. "Dorothy!" he cried. "Dorothy!"

Dorothy lurched forward off her chair, collapsed in a bloody death on the floor. The man hurled himself upon her. Wentworth

From below the platform-edge, Wentworth's bullet drilled up through the man's head.

spun toward the door leading into the warehouse. Somewhere here, he knew suddenly, he would find a clue to the cause of these fiendish deaths.

At the door, he paused. "If you value your lives," he snapped, "don't smoke anything. That's what killed the girl."

He shoved out through the door. Vast shadows lay all about him. Light filtered through dusty high windows dimly, emphasizing the darkness that lay in the corners and between the stacked pyramids of boxes. The air was full of the rich aroma of tobacco. It was aromatic and good to smell. Sniffing, Wentworth stopped and stared about him. Mingled with the tobacco scent was another odor, sour and slightly nauseous. It made his nostrils twitch. Slowly, his eyes narrowed. He had detected that odor before now. He realized abruptly that the same sour odor had been present in Steve's shop on that night when men had died.

A low curse grated in Wentworth's throat. That was it! Why hadn't he thought of it before? That sour smell was what the rats had fled, what that cat had fled in Steve Jardin's tobacco shop. That sour smell was what spelled death to those who smoked tobacco, but it was not the death itself. He had sniffed it and lived. There was tension throughout his strong, tall body as he strode on tight-muscled legs about the warehouse, flashing his pocket lamp into dark corners, prodding about stacked wooden boxes.

He was not quite sure what it was he sought, but if those rats had fled this odor a few minutes before, they had fled something occurring at that moment. In other words, whatever caused this sickish, hellish odor must still be somewhere near.

Finally, in a dark corner near the office, he found a smashed spring water bottle had spread liquid darkness over the floor. Here, the nauseous sour odor caught at his chest, wrenched at his stomach as if to pull it up through his throat. Wentworth retreated, bound a handkerchief over his mouth and nose and went back, to gather up a sample of the liquid. Even as he worked, the last moist drop evaporated into the air.

Wentworth thrust erect, whirled and raced to the office. "I'm placing an embargo on this warehouse," he snapped harshly. "Not so much as a pack of cigarettes is to be shipped out. Understand?"

The white-faced man was on his knees beside the body of the girl. He turned and his eyes had no understanding, only dumb suffering in their depths.

"Every ounce of tobacco in your warehouse is poisoned," Wentworth said. "That is what killed Dorothy. It will kill thousands of others if you allow it to go out."

The man's head sagged until his chin touched his chest. "It won't go out," he said heavily.

WENTWORTH HURRIED to the street. The street was dark save for the lights of his waiting taxi. Snow fell in close big flakes through the beams and formed globes of yellow glow about them. There was a calm purposefulness about the snow. It moved slowly, inevitably. There were small patches of it among the cobbles of the street. The walk was wet.

"That water bottle truck," said Wentworth. "Know where it went?"

The taxi driver straightened up, leaned forward and switched on the windshield wiper. It made heavy weather of the accumulated snow.

"Sure," he said. "Went straight ahead. Funny, every time they come out of a place, rats start coming out, too."

"Find that truck," Wentworth ordered as he climbed in. The taxi's headlights jumped out. In their path the snow seemed thicker than ever. It swirled as the cab moved forward, its motor muted, tires swishing on the wet cobbles. Wentworth leaned forward, straining his eyes against the shimmering wall of white. Street lights bloomed abruptly into brilliance, each picking up its moving haze of snow. Outside the spheres of light, the snow was invisible, but the housetops could be seen only through a mist.

"There, two blocks ahead," Wentworth said abruptly. The truck he trailed had showed for an instant beneath a street light, dragging its lumbering, snow-limned load on into the darkness. The taxi picked up speed, then slowed with its lamps spotlighting the parked truck. Two men were moving heavily toward a warehouse, each with a ten-gallon bottle on his shoulder.

Wentworth paid off the taxi driver and the cab spurted away. Suddenly he whirled, flung aside as he glimpsed a dark figure twenty feet away. Red powder-flame speared at him from that figure. Wentworth's gun leaped to his hand. The shots were muffled, wrapped in a soft blanket of snow. Twice more the dark figure fired and Wentworth felt a bullet pluck through his overcoat's skirt, heard a spring bottle crash, then liquid gurgling and splashing to the street.

Wentworth had fired three times, knew that his bullets had

struck, yet the man still crouched against the wall and blasted shots at him! Deliberately, Wentworth lifted his gun and fired again, this time at the head. The man lurched suddenly to the pavement. Wentworth sped toward him on light feet, gun ready in his fist.

The opening of a door came to his ears dimly and he laid his body flat along the wall, saw the two men rush out of the warehouse and throw themselves into the protection of the truck. An automobile engine muttered and another car loomed suddenly from the haze of snow.

Guns began to speak from the truck and the car together. Lead splashed against the brick wall where Wentworth crouched, ground along the pavement at his feet. With a smothered cry, he hurled himself at the body of the man he had shot, wormed between it and the wall.

Lead continued to chip the bricks. He heard it thump wetly into the body before him, felt the jerk and quiver of the dead flesh. The headlight glare passed and darkness squeezed in upon Wentworth—darkness that moved with the black specks of the falling snow. He crawled across the walk to the gutter, saw two men leap from the auto and join those upon the truck. Then both car and truck were trundling away into the twisting wraiths of snow.

WENTWORTH SPRANG to his feet and sprinted. He caught the truck as it lurched into third gear, swung up on its bottle-stacked back and clung there panting. The bottles rattled and thumped, empties. The gurgle of others that were full was deep and throaty. Wentworth did not dare use his light, but he fumbled over the necks of the bottles, found the one that the killer's bullets had smashed. He dipped his hand into the sloshing liquid and sniffed. His lips snarled back flat against his teeth. It was the same sour smell that had pervaded the warehouse—and ahead were four men who were dealing out this fearful death potion. Little did they know that the Spider was their passenger. Wentworth's grin grew fierce. They would find it out in good time—when they had led him to the hide-out of their master!

The truck lurched around a corner, headed westward. A few lighted widows began to show, dirty yellow shop windows with their scallops of frost and steam, then, finally, the curtained windows of homes. Street lights slid past and were instantly swallowed in the swarming snow. The boom of an elevated train came faintly, drew nearer and flashed past in a chain of hazed lights. The truck jerked to a stop.

The four men jumped off, and huddled together, moved in a bunch for the elevated steps. Wentworth hesitated a moment, then he jerked out a fountain pen, squeezed out the ink and flushed it a half-dozen times in the liquid of the broken bottle before filling it with the sour stinking stuff. Then he sprang down and went up the stairs to the elevated station also. The train had just gone past and save for the agent behind his lighted pane, a block of wood shutting out drafts through the change opening, save for the huddled four who had preceded him, Wentworth found the high platform deserted.

The snow had made little piles on the ties. The rails were wet and black. Wentworth stood aloof and stared at the lights of the platform across the tracks, but he kept watch out of the tail of his eye on the four men. He saw them separate, two strolling casually toward his back, the other two drifting down on his flank. He cursed softly and felt his jaw muscles tighten. How had they spotted him? No matter, it was obvious they had. His plan to follow them to headquarters was a failure even before he began to put it into operation. And might very well pay with his life for his brashness. It was doubtful that these men would be anxious to take a prisoner.

He slid his hand to the reloaded automatic beneath his arm. The four were almost upon him now, fists thrust into their coat pockets. In a moment they would stab him with a cross-fire of their ready weapons.

"Hey, buddy," one of the men said in a thick voice. "Give us a light, will you?"

Instead of turning to face the men, Wentworth stepped forward and dropped over the edge of the platform. He landed with a foot on each of two cross-ties, knees bent, guns flying to his hands. Instantly he whirled, crouched and stared upward. He was below the platform's edge. If they leaned over to fire at him....

Almost instantly a man did that, revolver pointed downward. Wentworth's bullet drilled up through his face, spattered his brains in the snow. The man's head jerked up, then he collapsed, pitching downward to the rails.

Wentworth caught the man as he fell, jerked him upright and shoved his face with its gaping wound into view above the edge of the platform. Guns blazed. The body quivered in his grasp. Wentworth let out a despairing cry, let the body fall and crouched to wait. He could hear the station agent yelling excitedly into a telephone; hear windows slamming up in nearby buildings. The rail over which he crouched began to hum. Another elevated train was coming.

HIS WAIT was futile. No gangster showed head or hand over the edge of the platform. Abruptly, Wentworth whirled about. Feet had crunched on the platform across the way. Even as he spun, guns began to flame there. He sent his own lead singing a vicious answer. One man screamed and pitched down. Snow wavered over the tracks. The figures of the men were vague. Their guns searched for him in vain.

Then he saw one man leap to the tracks from the opposite platform, jerked about to see another drawing a bead on him from behind. He snapped a shot over his shoulder, felt a jar of lead numb his left hand. One automatic dropped from his grasp, slithered between the ties to the street below. He crouched, ran along the edge of the platform, saw the shadow across the tracks paralleling his course. He snapped another shot at it, but the man ran on.

Between them was the width of two sets of rails, a three-foot gap between them. Besides each track was the third rail, charged with many volts of electricity. At the station, this was covered by a wooden box that protected workers against an accidental touch that would mean instant death. When the station was past, the cover disappeared.

It was a strange ghostly battle fought there on the elevated structure. Swirling snow made every shadow alive. The snow-wet ties were like slippery clay beneath the feet, and the black

104

menace of the charged third rail was at each man's elbow. The humming of the rails was louder now, but a bend hid the approaching train.

Wentworth fired again at a moving shadow on the opposite tracks and lead buzzed at him from the platform he had left There was a sand box there, placed in the station so the agent could use it on slippery platforms, and one gangster had crouched behind that. He was out of reach, but this other persistent shadow that slipped along on his right, what protected him? Wentworth recalled that the other assassin of the warehouse street had not fallen until he had fired at the head. The answer was simple—bullet-proof vests. But he could not see this assailant clearly enough to fire at the head.

He crouched, waited while the rails sang and the two bloody eyes of the elevated train's nose swung around the corner. Wentworth cursed. The train would stop before it reached the point where he crouched, but he must move fast if he would avoid its betraying light and be clear when it started off again. His lips thinned. It wouldn't start off again. That killer's body on the rail would tie it here until the corpse could be moved.

Wentworth sprang erect and raced down the ties toward the darkness. He stumbled, slipping on wet wood, nearly fell. Behind him, he heard a hoarse cry of anger. He whirled to see a man leap to the rail and follow. With an eager laugh, Wentworth ran on. He peered to his left. Springing along agilely on the other tracks, was the man he had tried a half-dozen times to kill. He was still only a blur. Wentworth raised his gun, then hesitated. He had only two cartridges left in this clip. There was no time to reload.

Behind there was a hissing discharge of air as the train slid to a halt. The ties were quivering beneath his feet. The shadow on his left was ahead of him now. He could make out the man against the hazing of a street light below. As he watched, the man stepped cautiously over the third rail, started toeing across a heavy steel support beam toward where Wentworth was.

Wentworth was trapped between the two gangsters. Below, he heard the eerie whine of a police siren as a radio prowl car answered the alarm of the station agent's call. The train back there—. The ties quivered beneath his feet again. What the hell! Had they moved the body already? He jerked to his left, found another of the steel cross beams which completely spanned the street and cautiously stepped over the third rail. Fifty feet away, he made out the figure of the gangster, sidling across another similar beam. Grimly, Wentworth eased himself to a seat on the steel. He rested his automatic in the crotch of his arm and sent one last bullet winging toward the gangster.

HE SAW the shadow waver, arms flung high, heard a shrill, high-pitched scream. But the gangster did not fall. He tottered nearer to the tracks over which the train was once more grinding. He seemed to be doing a weird dance on the air. Abruptly, he pitched forward and there was a blinding flash of blue-white flame. It dissolved the haze of snow, showed the gangster in black silhouette, hands wrapped in the electric fire of the third rail! As suddenly as it had risen, darkness flopped back on the scene and a soft thud from the street told the fate of the gangster.

Wentworth whirled to find the second hood bounding along frantically in front of the oncoming train. A gun glinted in his hand and as he ran, he edged nearer and nearer to the third rail. He had already passed the last transverse. He could not retreat to it because of the train and his only hope was to reach the beam where Wentworth crouched. And Wentworth waited there with his automatic ready and a tight grin on his lips.

The killer was in a good light now, outlined by the lights of the train. Once more Wentworth rested his automatic on his arm. He heard the hiss of air as the elevated train again put on brakes. At that instant, he fired. The gangster staggered. The gun flew from his grasp and his right arm dropped limply to his side. Instantly, Wentworth sprang across the third rail and seized him by the coat collar.

He swung him back toward the train. From the station platform, he heard hoarsely shouted orders. The police had climbed to the station now, but they were fifty yards behind the train, which effectually prevented their reaching him. He pushed the hood to the front of the train, scrambled up on the coupling pin and over the iron railing of the platform, hauling the gangster up with him.

The man slumped down on the floor, groaning with the pain of his arm. Wentworth yanked open the front door of the car. Men and women were standing in the aisles, staring forward with frightened faces. Wentworth waved his gun, shoving the gangster ahead of him.

"It's all right," he told them. "I'm a cop. This crook tried to get away."

The door of the motorman's cubicle opened. Wentworth thrust the gun against the operator's ribs.

"Get moving," he snapped. "And don't bother about station stops."

The motorman gaped at him, breathing hoarsely through his mouth. Wentworth jabbed him gently in the throat with the gun muzzle.

"Get the train moving," he ordered again.

The train started with a lurch that half threw the people in the aisles off their feet. Wentworth clung grimly to his position. He knew that the police would pursue within minutes after the train's start, but they would have to get down the station stairs and get their cars started. He would gain a few more moments there, but afterward it would be a losing race. The lumbering, dilapidated wooden trains could not make more than fifteen or twenty miles an hour under the best of conditions. And this was night and snowing hard. The police car could do sixty or sixty-five, once it got started.

TEN BLOCKS along the route, after two stations had been passed without stops, Wentworth made the motorman halt the train just around a curve, made him carry the wounded gangster down the length of three cars. They shoved out beside the cars, onto the tie butts on the inside of the curve. Then he sent the motorman back to take the train away. The operator lost no time. The elevated creaked and groaned on into the darkness. It was rounding another turn six blocks away when the police sirened their way past beneath the structure.

Swiftly then, Wentworth looped his silken rope beneath

the man's arms and lowered him over
the side to the walk. Then he took
the doubled line in his hands and
slid down to join him. The man was
stumbling, seemed scarcely able to
stand though the wound in his arm
had not even fractured it. Wentworth

clung to him grimly. There were certain questions he wanted to
ask this assassin who had helped distribute the poison that was
killing thousands.

He gripped him by his good arm and reeled a little as if they
both were drunken. They made a weaving way down the walk
to find a taxi. A heavy black car was lounging along beneath
the elevated structure. It swerved suddenly to the wrong side
of the street and four men sprang from the tonneau. One held
a sawed-off shotgun, another a machine gun. The other two
held revolvers and one of them sauntered up to Wentworth and
bowed sardonically.

"If you gentlemen will deign enter our unworthy car," he
murmured, "the favor would be much appreciated."

Wentworth stared into the man's face, saw the dull glitter
of his slant eyes. A Chinese! His glance flew to the others who
stood alertly ready, shotgun and machine gun poised. Not a
chance to escape. He'd be dropped before he took two steps,
before he could fire more than one shot… A gay smile twisted
his lips. Well, perhaps, he would meet the leader of these hellish
killers before they took him out to die.

"With pleasure," he murmured. "We were just looking for a car. Yours will do as well as any other."

The Chinese who had bowed did not smile. He nodded his head gravely, held the door open. As Wentworth stepped in, the Oriental slugged him heavily with the automatic, and blackness blotted out his mind.

CHAPTER 11
THE CRIMSON VEIL

THE GROANS Wentworth heard did not sound as if they could be human. They were followed by an animal whimpering. The moaning penetrated through the gray and black veil that clung like cobwebs to his brain. He forced his eyes open, shut them again with a shudder. Was he in hell? He shifted his hands, found they were bound together at his back. Then memory flooded back.

He opened his eyes furtively a second time. A Chinese, stripped to the skin, lay bound to a table. About him were grouped four dark forms, but they were in shadow. The only light was the brilliant white cone that burned down upon the prisoner from a hanging lamp. It was from the naked Chinese that the moans and whimperings came. Abruptly, Wentworth understood the reason. One of those four dark forms lifted his hand and a piece of steel glowed white hot in the gloom.

The white hot steel vanished behind the body of the man that held it. An agonized shriek burst from the prisoner. He writhed against his bonds, muscles quivering with pain spasms.

110

To Wentworth's nostrils came a nauseous stench—burning human flesh. A tremor shook him. His arms strained against his bonds.

"Come, Ming," a hissing, Oriental voice said, "or I shall cease to be gentle with you? Tell us the secret... or perhaps you prefer to lose the other eye, too?"

Anger surged up through Wentworth, anger that brought with it a cold touch of stark fear. We he, too, destined for that torture table?

"I assure you," the expressionless voice went on, "the work will be done aseptically. Heat is a great purifier. See—" Another tearing shriek ripped from the wretch upon the table. "Why, Ming, you are most ungrateful!"

Suddenly a slobbering jargon of sounds gushed from the man on the table, a hurried outpour of a frantic singsong dialect.

"Talk English," the speaker admonished. "How do you expect us to understand your outrageous northern dialect?"

"I have told you all I know," the prisoner gasped. "The liquid in some of the bottles turns to gas. That poisons the tobacco. I do not know how it is made. My master is the Red Mandarin, but I do not know who he is save that he is a searer of the five-toed dragon."

Breath hissed sharply from the assembled men. They gargled and grunted in sing-song Chinese. One of them reached down the torture iron toward the glow of the brazier where it had been heated. The iron missed it and clattered to the floor, but the man did not seem to notice. A cold smile twisted Wentworth's mouth. It would soon be his turn. The iron still glowed brightly, though it was dulling to red.

While the Chinese chattered busily among themselves, Wentworth slipped his bound feet toward the iron. For a moment he fumbled, then he wedged the rod between his heels and began to slide it toward him. He could reach only the hot end and the heat of it seeped through the leather of his shoes. The scent of scorched leather reached his nostrils.

Abruptly the chatter ceased. The men apparently had reached some decision, for they turned back to their prisoner. The one who had wielded the torture-iron drew a knife. A cry of terror rang out, then a groan. Once more the body threshed upon the table. Wentworth could see by the hunching of the knife-man's shoulders that he was thrusting the blade in slowly.

The screams of the man on the table would drown out the scraping of the torture-iron. It was cooling rapidly. There would be no heat in it by the time the ropes about his wrists could reach it. But already, it was eating into the bonds of his ankles. He ceased his efforts to pull the bar to his wrists and sawed the ankle ropes. The smell of burning rope mingled with the nauseous stenches that already filled the room.

THE WRITHINGS of the man on the table became a convulsive kicking; then that, too, ceased. Wentworth felt the rope about his ankles part, saw the men step back from the table. Instantly, he was upon his feet. What chance did he have with his arms bound behind him, unarmed against four torturers? Wentworth could not permit himself to think of that. He knew now how the death that was striking down thousands of innocent human beings was meted out because of some deep-laid sinister plan. He must get free and warn the public—have the dangerous tobacco destroyed. It was not Wentworth alone who fought here for his life tonight; the fate of tens of millions of innocent Americans was involved.

As he sprang to his feet, the Chinese whirled with startled cries. The hand of one flashed to his hip. Wentworth's eyes flew wide in amazement. The man wore a crimson veil that hid his entire face, a perfect mask that did not reveal even the eyes of the wearer. The man was silhouetted against the light now and he was thin and tall like a skeleton in clothes!

Wentworth's breath hissed out and rage flamed within him. He did not wait for the attack. He sprang forward and slammed his foot against the charcoal brazier.

Immediately, white-hot coals spattered over the room. Men danced away from the embers howling. Another bound put Wentworth beside the table. He seized the rim of the light shade in his teeth, clenched savagely, hurled his weight backward.

His teeth felt as if they were being yanked from his head. Blood seeped from his torn gums and his mouth was full of warm, sticky saltiness. He shook his head violently from side to side, wrenched again. The shade pulled loose from its fastenings, pinched the light bulb and crushed it with a muffled pop. Broken fragments of glass pricked Wentworth's face. He went backward to the floor, doubled forward and crept beneath the torture table.

He opened his mouth so that his whistling breath might not betray him and crouched waiting. His battle to extinguish the light had lasted less than two seconds—two precious seconds gained while the Chinese danced away from the burning coals. Now those spots of sizzling white spread an eerie glow in the darkness of the floor. But they were fading rapidly, graying into coldness.

One of the Chinese, sang out a splutter of words. Wentworth heard slippered feet encircling the spot where he crouched. A door opened and closed. A grim smile twisted his bloody lips. One man had gone for more help, as if it were needed! Still he had a chance. He had noticed in that instant before the light went out that the knife still rested, almost hilt deep, in the chest of the tortured Chinese. If he could reach that....

Wentworth crept out from beneath the table, stood with his back to the body and tried to find the knife. His hands barely came above the table's edge; Sweat popped out on his forehead as he struggled to stretch his arms out farther, to reach that blade which meant the life of thousands. It was useless. He eased himself up to a seat on the side of the table, drew his feet up under him and inched on until he sat upon the stomach of the dead Chinese. The flesh was clammy and chilling beneath him. Its softness was horrible.

Slowly, then, Wentworth hunched up the body of the dead Chinese. Suddenly he froze, horror crawling up his spine. A hoarse, formless groan wheezed from the corpse! The sound brought squeals of fear from two of the Chinese in the darkness. It jerked at Wentworth's muscles too, but he knew the answer. His weight had squeezed air from the dead man's lungs, had caused the sound. That was all, but it was horrible.

HE INCHED on and abruptly his hands closed on the hilt of the knife. He eased it half way from the wound, then sawed the ropes rapidly against the edge of the blade. In seconds, they parted, but he did not at once climb down from his gruesome perch. Three of the Chinese were still in the room, waiting for the return of that other man they had dispatched. What weapon had that one gone for? Wentworth weighed the knife across his palm and waited. The darkness he could understand. His captors did not know what weapon he held, probably had not detected in those brief moments of light the fact that his hands were still bound.

But his position, seated upon the table, was too exposed. He eased to the floor and as he did it, the dead Chinese groaned again. A new whimper of fright from the darkness answered that.

Crouching beside the table, Wentworth put both hands on the corpse and pressed another rasping moan from it. There was a gleam in his eye. He imitated the sound in his own throat, more loudly, again, then he spoke in sepulchral tones: "You may bind my body. You cannot bind my ghost. I have come for vengeance!"

Dead silence greeted the words.

"The knife and the torture iron," Wentworth continued in a voice that was half a groan. "They shall strike for me."

Groping on the floor, Wentworth found the iron rod which had fallen to the floor. He picked it up, whirled it once about his head and hurled it whistling through the air. It thudded against flesh and a man screamed shrilly. Slippered feet slapped across the room. A door creaked open and a pistol streaked flame toward that sound. The man who had fled screamed again, moaned, thudded to the floor. The door creaked shut again.

"Do not think, fool, that you can scare me with your tricks," a man whispered. "I know the dead do not rise. You shall die, even as that coward died."

Wentworth answered with another groan. The fact that he had not fired back at the flash of the other assailant's gun gave the man courage. He sped a bullet toward Wentworth and Wentworth, crouched behind the corpse, laughed shrilly.

"Shoot! Shoot my body!" he cackled. "It will not save you."

He was sawing at the ropes that held the corpse to the table. He cut the last one, took the body by upper arm and thigh and heaved it violently from him toward the flash. The body thudded. A man cursed and there was a confused scrambling.

Wentworth charged the sound, his knife poised across his palm. He rammed against a staggering man, flung his left arm in a sweeping blow to fend off a possible shot and thrust forward and upward viciously with the knife. It met resistance and he shoved it home, left the blade sheath in flesh. His left arm had struck another man and a gun blasted harmlessly at his side. He jerked out the knife and struck again with it. The man fell away from the thrust and went down, threshing.

Wentworth flung himself down beside the corpse. The door rattled, swung open, and the room blazed with light from a magnesium flare. Wentworth covered his eyes, spotted the glint of the automatic whose owner he had knifed. He snatched it up. For the moment, the light favored him equally with these other two who still lived. He fired blindly behind the light and saw the flare arc to the floor. He pivoted, blazed away again at the spot from which the last shot had come.

Blasting gun fire answered and lead smacked against the wall behind him. The ceiling of the room seemed to swell upward with the sound, then crash back about his ears. He flung to the floor, arm shielding his face against the light glare and made out movement—a man charging toward the door. He flung up his gun and this time it spat death. The man slammed down. His face struck the flare and it sputtered for a few moments against dying flesh that was too far gone to scream with pain.

WENTWORTH REELED weakly to his feet. He found his pocket flashlight and its disc of light flickered over the room. Moisture glistened on concrete walls. Not a sound penetrated. Obviously this chamber of tortures was subterranean, probably a sub-cellar. Wentworth examined the bodies swiftly, found and bolstered his guns; found also that the four men he had slain carried in their pockets cards of the Star of the East detective agency. Also, on two forearms, he found the five-claw dragon brand. The man of the Crimson Veil had escaped.

Frowning thoughtfully, Wentworth affixed his blood-red seal on all the men except the tortured one, then he made his way to the door. His flashlight revealed the accuracy of his guess as to the location of this room. He climbed two flights of stairs, found himself in a murky areaway between two dark buildings. He slipped out to the street; found that he was on the East Side in a tenement district on the fringe of Chinatown.

As he stood, glancing warily about, he saw the gliding shadows of Orientals merging with the darkness of building fronts, vanishing into black doorways. The air had warmed and the drifting snow had turned to a fine rain that already had washed the streets clean of slush. Water drip splashed from the cornices of buildings, glistened blackly under the distant brush of street lights.

Wentworth knew his next move must be to trace down the Star of the East detective agency. He did not think it was responsible for the wholesale killings which were terrifying New York, but somewhere there was a link between the activities of the two groups. And there no longer was any doubt that the murders were directed by Chinese. He turned his collar up against the rain and, slouching his shoulders, pushed on through the cold rain. He stopped to mail the fountain pen full of the gas death-liquid to Professor Brownlee, then hunted up a telephone book. It revealed the location of the offices of the detective agency. He had little difficulty slipping unobserved into the building, and burglarizing the offices. But even the confidential files from the safe revealed nothing that might be called a clue. He restored everything to its original condition and left.

His next call was on the offices of the Denict Company which advertised that its cigarettes were safe. He could find nothing to connect the company with Chinese or the East. He left wearily, and riding the subway, bought a paper from a grimy-faced newsboy. A box on the front page said: *Three more days to Christmas!* Wentworth smiled wanly. Christmas would bring only sorrow and despair to hundreds of homes this year.

He glanced at the headlines and his hands, gripping the

paper, tensed. Deacon Coslin was making more predictions. The next to suffer from the "vengeance of the Lord," Coslin said, would be those who drank coffee and liquor, who danced and attended theatres. He predicted many more would die before the Lord wearied of chastising the sinners. Remembering with what fearful carnage the man's previous prophecies had been fulfilled, Wentworth felt a cold dread working its way into the very marrow of his bones. It was replaced with a narrow-eyed anger. It was not possible that the man should foretell happenings so accurately unless he had some guilty knowledge of the preparations, or unless facts were communicated to him in his "dreams" as he said.

A sudden thought struck Wentworth. Many strange and apparently impossible things had happened since he had entered this battle with the Five-Clawed Dragon. Was it possible that someone was drugging Coslin and planting the germs of his visions in his brain to be remembered as divine prophecies when he awoke? Wentworth jerked his head impatiently. It seemed ridiculous, yet somehow he felt that the clue to all his search centered somehow about the cultist's obnoxious personality. He resolved to search him out, keep a watch over him and seek to learn the secret of the prophecies. But first he had another grimmer business to attend to—the poisoned tobacco. It must be destroyed before it spread more death among the people.

In the paper were new ads of the Denict Tobacco Company. There also were ads for "safe" liquors and "safe" coffees. Wentworth's eyes tightened. He wondered angrily if Coslin had stock in the companies. But he had found no proof of that in the

Denict offices. He read on. An entire inner page of the paper was given over to agate lists of names of those who had perished on the previous day and the number ran above five thousand.

Wentworth cursed. Chicago, too, had felt the strength of the hidden monster's hand! A dozen there had died of the strange malady and police had appealed to New York for help in combating the "epidemic." Damn it, couldn't anyone see the truth of the matter, that poison was killing the people?

Wentworth balled the paper into a knot, hurled it at a trash can as he strode from the subway. Kirkpatrick knew the truth. He, Wentworth, had told him. Yet he permitted these lies to be fostered and grow. It was time that there was a showdown on the issue. The Spider would pay a call on his erstwhile friend, the Commissioner of Police.

CHAPTER 12
KIRKPATRICK
RECEIVES A CALLER

THE STREET lights winked out when the dawn was still a purple glimmer in the east, before the sickly gray of winter morning poked feeble fingers of light among the canyons of the city. Working men were already astir, for the December sun comes late. They trooped, heavy-footed, along the rousing streets, short-stemmed pipes between their teeth, shapeless caps drawn down to meet the turned-up collars of their soggy mackinaws. The rain had finished, leaving an edge like glittering ice to the air. Wentworth parked his car, strode past the clopping workmen with his brisk swinging pace. He had stripped off all disguise and the beaten weariness of his face was—clearly visible in the tautness about his drawn mouth, in the hardness about his gleaming eyes. He carried himself erectly, but there was an alert forward thrust to his shoulders as if he walked into battle and was eager for the clash of arms.

He turned into Fifth Avenue and swung into the door of Kirkpatrick's apartment house. He nodded casually to the policeman on guard and the man touched his club to his visor. A smile just touched Wentworth's lips and faded. Wentworth was a hunted man but because he did not look furtive, because he spoke openly to the policeman, he did not excite suspicion. The hall boy awaited his approach respectfully.

"Mr. Kirkpatrick's apartment," said Wentworth. "I'm expected."

The man nodded respectfully and took Wentworth up. It was considerate of Kirkpatrick to have taken this apartment for the winter, Wentworth thought. It spared him that long trip uptown. The butler opened the door to his ring, started to bow, then stared. He retreated three swift backward paces, turned and fled.

"I say, Francis," Wentworth called after him, "would you mind telling your master I'm here?"

The slight smile still played about his mouth. The butler was better up on detail than the police, it seemed. He knew that Wentworth was a hunted man and his appearance at his master's quarters meant trouble. Wentworth sauntered on into the apartment, tossed hat and cane casually to a table and folded his overcoat across a chair. He was in the act of lighting a cigarette when Kirkpatrick stormed into the room with a revolver in his hand, his hair still rumpled from sleep, a bathrobe bound about him by a knotted cord.

"This is nice of you, Wentworth," he said coldly. "You've spared me a lot of trouble."

Wentworth finished lighting the cigarette he had placed between his lips, gray-blue eyes flicking over Kirkpatrick's taut body. The revolver was not pointed but held ready at the Commissioner's side; his legs were braced wide apart and the tendons of his feet, bare in house slippers, were visible evidence of his tension. Wentworth snapped the flame from his cigarette lighter, pocketed it and smiled.

"I appreciate the compliment of your haste, Kirk," he said easily. "It is the first time you have ever received me without stopping to comb your hair."

Kirkpatrick glowered at him with his head thrust forward. His mustaches were bushy, without their usual smooth waxed perfection.

"What did you come here for?" Kirkpatrick demanded.

Wentworth was aware that the butler was talking in urgent low tones over a phone, probably calling the policeman up from the first floor; he was aware, too, that hatred glared at him from the eyes of his friend. He turned his shoulder on Kirkpatrick, strolled over to a davenport and lounged on it, crossing his knees. "DO YOU know, Kirkpatrick," he said casually, "that every move you make is helping the murderers who are killing the city's people by thousands?"

Kirkpatrick kept up his uncompromising glare, said nothing.

"There isn't any doubt any longer," Wentworth continued, "that the poison is spread through tobacco. I can even tell you how it's put into the cigarettes. A fake delivery truck of a spring water company goes about and spills a liquid in the warehouses. This forms a gas that gets into the tobacco and poisons it. The gas itself apparently isn't poison because I sniffed it and didn't die."

Kirkpatrick said woodenly: "It isn't poison that kills the people. Our chemists have found no poison in the bodies or the tobacco."

Wentworth frowned at him, studying his friend's stiff poise. What the hell was wrong with Kirkpatrick? Ordinarily he would have been the first to seize upon such information, but now he merely repeated this parroted information that was leading thousands daily to their deaths. He stared directly into Kirkpatrick's eyes and a start of surprise jerked at his muscles. Outwardly he still smiled, but a horror began to grow within him.

This man who had been his friend intended to kill him.

Wentworth could not doubt it. He had seen it in Kirkpatrick's eyes as clearly as if the Police Commissioner had spoken his purpose aloud. What in God's name was the matter? Had Kirkpatrick gone mad? Or worse, had he formed an alliance with the murderous monster who was decimating the city's population?

Wentworth shook his head, still smiling. That was impossible. Whatever else happened, Kirkpatrick would not ally himself with the forces of the underworld. Yet here was the evidence of refusing to take the obvious steps which would help to checkmate the killers. And here, too, was the evidence before his eyes that Kirkpatrick planned to kill him. He saw the rigidity of that purpose creep into Kirkpatrick's right arm, saw the hand tensing about the revolver and abruptly, Wentworth uncrossed his knees, put both feet on the floor and leaped forward.

The gun came up like a streak, but Wentworth went in under it. His shoulder caught Kirkpatrick in the stomach as the revolver blasted and together they went over and back, crashing into a table, spilling it to the floor with a thunder of broken glass and tumbling bric-a-brac. The lamp smashed and half-darkness slapped down on the room, leaving only the gray light of early day sifting in through the windows. The butler squealed in the hallway.

As they went down, Wentworth jerked up his left arm and grabbed for the revolver. A second shot brought down a white powder of plaster from the ceiling. Then Wentworth's fingers wrapped about Kirkpatrick's wrist. His right hand groped and thrust upward under Kirkpatrick's chin. He grunted as left-handed blows rained on his body. A knee thumped upward toward his groin. Unshod feet struck at him. Kirkpatrick was fighting furiously. Wentworth leaped abruptly to his feet, hauling Kirkpatrick upward also by his grip on the gun wrist. As the Police Commissioner came erect, Wentworth pivoted, went under that right arm, twisted it around behind Kirkpatrick. He thrust out his right hand and twisted Kirkpatrick's head so that he could not writhe out of the hammerlock. They stood rigidly like that, straining muscle against muscle and Wentworth's eyes were still narrowed with the death-horror that swelled within him. This all seemed utterly unreal. Here he was fighting with his best, almost his only, friend—fighting for his life against a deliberate attempt at murder!

BUT THIS must end quickly. He could hear the butler squealing into the telephone, could hear the beat of a nightstick on the door. With an abrupt change of tactics, he seized Kirkpatrick's wrist with both hands and twisted the gun from his grasp. As it came free he palmed it and slapped his friend soundly behind the ear. Kirkpatrick went down on his hands and knees, swayed a moment and clumped flat on his face.

In three long leaps, Wentworth crossed the room and crouched beside the entrance. The outer door swung open. He heard the policeman curse, heard his feet slap forward. Then, as the man came through the door, Wentworth struck again and connected. He bounded past the falling man and seized the butler, dropped him with a right to the jaw. His breath was coming fast between clenched teeth. A tight frown knotted his forehead, drew his smooth black brows down over his eyes.

Slowly, with weighted steps he crossed to the door and closed it, moving like a man in a daze. He shook his head violently and drove himself into action, but the frown remained. He found picture wire and adhesive and bound the butler and policeman, gagged them. He rapidly donned the policeman's coat and visored cap, then he crossed to Kirkpatrick and, heaving him up from the floor, carried him to his bedroom.

The Police Commissioner rallied rapidly under his ministrations, and while he still fought his way back from unconsciousness to full use of his senses, Wentworth herded him into clothing. He shaved off Kirkpatrick's mustache swiftly and put his own hat and coat upon him, handcuffed him with the officer's manacles.

Kirkpatrick swore at him steadily, with a venom that first chilled, then aroused a slow heat of anger within Wentworth. There was something terribly wrong here—something that had planted a murderous fury in his friend's brain. Wentworth's mind flew back to the days when a false Spider had deliberately made it seem that Wentworth murdered a policeman and loosed a fearful scourge upon the city. Even then Kirkpatrick had not been able to believe in his friend's guilt. Yet now, when there was practically no evidence at all, Kirkpatrick suspected him, refused to help put down the criminals, and even attempted open murder.

Wentworth yanked Kirkpatrick to his feet, thrust him toward the outer door of the apartment. He paused there for a moment, stripped adhesive across Kirkpatrick's mouth, wedging him against the wall with a forearm on his throat. Then he wrapped a muffler high over his nose to hide it. Afterward he herded his friend out of the apartment and into the elevator.

The operator goggled at them, but Wentworth kept his face down and did not speak except to curse harshly and threaten Kirkpatrick with his club when the Commissioner tried to break loose and show his gagged mouth. Wentworth had to fight Kirkpatrick through the lobby and into a taxi.

"Headquarters," he barked at the driver.

Eight blocks away, he stopped the cab and ordered the driver away. The man stared back and Wentworth cursed softly. He could see that the man was suspicious. He would pick up the first cop he saw and come hurrying back. Luckily, Wentworth's car was only a half block away. He hustled Kirkpatrick along, almost carrying him bodily, thrust him into the car and stepped on the starter. The engine coughed, backfired. It did that three times before it caught and they jerked into motion.

A HALF hour later, Wentworth had Kirkpatrick in a side-street boarding house, stretched upon a bed with feet and hands handcuffed to the four posts. He left him like that until he got in touch with Ram Singh at his apartment and ordered him here to stand guard. Police had ceased to guard the apartment, and he had little trouble in reaching his servant. Ram Singh stared impassively down at the fuming Kirkpatrick.

"Outside the door," Wentworth instructed, "is a telephone. Until you hear from me, keep him a prisoner here like this."

Ram Singh bowed, cupped hands going to his forehead. *"Han, sahib!"* he assented.

"You have not been followed?"

"I was, *sahib,*" Ram Singh said slowly, "but only for a brief while."

Wentworth smiled coldly. He could trust the Hindu with his own life. He could trust him to obey orders regardless of Kirkpatrick's threats.

Wentworth left the boarding house. It was noon and the cold sunlight gleamed weakly on the streets. Men walked with their shoulders hunched, their breath a plume before their faces. This kidnapping of Kirkpatrick had taken longer than he expected. He could only hope that the warehouse man had obeyed his embargo of words upon the sale of tobacco. If he had respected it until now, Wentworth would take of the future. He smiled coldly. It was not often that his actions harmed the innocent, but today he must commit a crime to prevent greater crimes. He would commit arson to prevent countless murders. The purifying tongue of fire would consume the poisoned tobacco.

It was characteristic of Wentworth that he chose the major crime for himself and left Ram Singh merely to guard Kirkpatrick. He strode swiftly along the street, drawing on gloves, his cane dangling from his arm. He might have been off to an afternoon in an art gallery instead of heading for a warehouse he meant to set on fire....

CHAPTER 13
FIRE PURIFICATION

WHEN HE reached the elevated station nearest the warehouse, he found that the spring water truck with its big ten-gallon bottles was still parked at the curb. A policeman had tagged it for parking all night without lights.

Wentworth laughed. He strode up Second Avenue until he found a clothing store where he bought overalls and a workman's short coat. He dressed in an elevated washroom, colored his face in imitation of a day-old beard and stuck the short stem of a pipe between his teeth. He grinned at himself in a cracked mirror.

"Sh-ure now 'tis the broth of a lad I'm after being," he muttered and stumped downstairs to the truck. He got it started after a while and rolled to a gasoline station where he had a number of the ten-gallon bottles filled with gasoline. The service man looked at him curiously but did not demur. He would have shouted for police could he have seen Wentworth, fifteen minutes later, carrying one of those bottles of gasoline into the warehouse where the day before poisoning gas had been loosed. Wentworth stumped past the office, through the door, and into the back storage room where the other bottle had been spilled. He put his down gingerly and looked around. The embargo apparently had been obeyed. Not a man was at work in the warehouse section.

Wentworth slopped the gasoline over the floor in a spreading lake of liquid, lighted a cigarette and flipped it. Hurriedly, he slammed through the door and ran to the office. The gasoline let go with an explosive gust. Black smoke billowed upward.

"Fire!" Wentworth yelled. "Fire! Clear out of here!"

There were four persons working in the office. They got out hurriedly and Wentworth waited to see that the last one was clear before he himself left the flaming building. There was a taut smile on his lips. If the warehouse were not burned to the ground, at least the goods within it would be too badly damaged to carry poison to innocent people.

While the street thronged with fire equipment, he ran his truck on to a second warehouse which the rats had fled, and this one also he set fire in the same manner. A suspicious office worker accused him, tried to hold him, but Wentworth punched him into unconsciousness, carried him from the burning building, put him down beside an ambulance.

"Smoke got him," he said, and hurried on to continue his work.

129

It was an hour after dark when Wentworth returned to the room where Kirkpatrick was a prisoner, relieving Ram Singh so that he could go out to dinner. Extras were being screamed in the streets. They told of new hundreds of death scattered throughout the country.

New York continued to lead in the grisly race. Fifteen hundred had been killed there. Doctors continued to be quoted that the deaths apparently were caused by tobacco. One scientist had a theory that the plant had turned malignant and that unknown poisons lurked in it. He talked vaguely of ultra-violet rays to kill the virus. Washington at last was taking cognizance of the affair and the Department of Justice was moving to slap an embargo on all tobacco until the matter was cleared up. Kirkpatrick's kidnapping screamed at him in black-faced type.

Another streamer shouted that the Spider had destroyed five warehouses with fire. He had telephoned the editor of the paper personally and told him the reason for this was that the tobacco had been poisoned. Deacon Coslin was quoted again at great length on his prophecies. Wentworth turned to find Kirkpatrick glowering at him.

"The Spider thinks as I do, Kirk," Wentworth said softly. "He

Nita Van Sloan

burned five warehouses this afternoon and phoned an editor that the tobacco was poisoned."

KIRKPATRICK'S FURIOUS eyes gave no answer. He couldn't speak because of the careful gag that Wentworth had contrived, but there was still murder in his glance—murderous rage that had nothing to do with his captivity. Wentworth shook his head slowly, frowning with worry. He was positive that something had affected his friend's mind, had turned him from his usual calm, keen self into a killing ally of criminals. Wentworth eyed Kirkpatrick speculatively. "I know you hate me now, Kirk," he said, "but believe me, I am still working for the good of the people. Tell me, do you know a Chinese named Wu Chang?"

Kirkpatrick glared at him, but finally he nodded. Wentworth leaned forward and ripped off his gag. "When did you meet him?" he demanded.

"On the night you made your first kills!" Kirkpatrick spat out the words and Wentworth sucked in his breath.

"Before or after?" he asked swiftly.

"Before, you murderer!" Kirkpatrick snapped. Suddenly he shouted hoarsely for help. Wentworth slapped his hand over his mouth, replacing the adhesive-tape gag. He threw back his head and bellowed hoarsely with laughter.

"That's a swell joke," he guffawed, made more of the hoarse shouting sounds. He listened intently. Apparently no one had taken alarm at Kirkpatrick's choked-off cry.

Wentworth arose heavily, went to the telephone, called Professor Brownlee to learn whether he had succeeded where other chemists had failed in analysis of the poison. Brownlee, in addition to his brilliant mind, had another advantage over the other chemists. He had the actual poison for test.

Brownlee's jerky, excited voice came over the wire. "I've got it, Dick!" he cried. "But I don't see how it will do you much good to know. It's a most ingenious thing. The gas itself is not poisonous, but what it does, apparently, is to multiply the power of other poisons. Thus the nicotine in a thousand cigarettes would not kill a man, but this gas has the power of building up the nicotine in one cigarette to the killing point. It would carry other effects, of course. There would be strangulation and nausea."

Wentworth nodded slowly in the dimness of the hall. "I suspected something of the sort and you have accurately described the symptoms," he told Professor Brownlee. "Do you have any suggestions for treatment?"

"Treatment is practically impossible," Brownlee said slowly. "Poisons that enter the system through the lungs are almost instantaneous. I am working to devise a gas which, coming in contact with tobacco already exposed to the poison, will neutralize it."

"Good," Wentworth said heartily. "Keep up the good work."

He hung up and the heartiness went out of him. There was no way to battle against the gas, no way to save the victims. There was only one thing to do—destroy the author of this infamy.

There was the man with the crimson veil and that one who called himself the Red Mandarin and branded his servitors with a five-clawed dragon's foot. He thought of the venerable Chinese Wu Chang, and of Deacon Coslin and his prophecies. Those two were next on his list.

Ram Singh returned and Wentworth sped directly to Coslin's home. He found it deserted save for the giant negroes who were the servants. The cultist, they said, was investigating nudity in the theaters this evening. He was attending a showing of the *Delights of 1934*. Wentworth's mocking brows lifted slightly at that information. Had not Deacon Coslin prophesied the death of theater-goers? Yet he braved his own predictions now to attend the most undressed review in town. The Chinese girl, Ya Che, he learned, had gone with him. One other thing Wentworth learned. The date of Wu Chang's "conversion" to the cult preceded by just two days the date of Deacon Coslin's first prediction of tobacco deaths. His mind flew back to what Kirkpatrick had said. Was it possible Wu Chang had used some fiendish eastern art to enslave him?

WENTWORTH STRODE from the house, sent his taxi spinning through the park and down Seventh Avenue toward the theater. He was frowning with thought. Wu Chang's arrival just before the predictions might be coincidence, of course, but he was an Oriental and there was more than a hint of Manchu in the appearance of his daughter, Ya Che. The five-clawed dragon symbol had last been used by the Manchu emperors. Coupled with that was Wentworth's conviction that Coslin had been drugged into these dreams in which the monstrous happenings of recent days were foretold. With Ya Che's help, it would not be difficult to trick him. Wu Chang and his lovely daughter were scheduled to receive a call from the Spider.

His taxi slid down Seventh Avenue. In Times Square, he blinked his eyes at a tall cedar tree festooned with brilliant electric lights. He recalled with a start that this was Christmas Eve! Good heavens, Christmas Eve and the gaunt murderer, the skeleton man with his crimson veil, stalked the streets in a murderous frenzy, outdoing even the Grim Reaper himself.

Wentworth stared about him with fear-sick eyes, his mind tortured by haggard worries. He and Nita had a long standing engagement for this night. They were going to do the thing up brown with the theater and a late dinner at Pierre's. They planned to finish up by hanging their stockings and socks before Nita's fireplace, closing their eyes while each played Santa Claus to the other. A bitter smile twisted his lips.

"Subject to cancellation without notice," he had told Nita blithely when they made that date.

Nita's great violet eyes had deepened and she had clung to him, but there had been a brave smile on her lips. "Who is this other woman?" she demanded in mock fierceness. "You're just paving the way to breaking our date."

"My intentions, my sweet, are of the best," he had protested.

Suddenly Nita had pressed her lips to his. "Hell is paved with those, I'm told," she had whispered, "and you're such a devil with the ladies."

Laughter rasped in Wentworth's throat. God alone knew where Nita was tonight. He could not even allow himself to think of her. There was work for the Spider and until that work was finished, duty would not permit him to turn from the battle of humanity to this private woe.

Somehow the gayety of Broadway seemed muted this Christmas Eve. There was a sodden warmth in the air that would shroud the harbor in fog, that already had blotted out the high lights of skyscraper towers. The flickering signs of red and blue and glaring green were lightly hazed. He glanced up at them when his taxi stalled in a streaming jam of crossing humanity. He noticed that one of the most famous signs of Times Square, that directly at Forty-Seventh street where the triangle of Long

Acre Square terminated the X where Broadway and Seventh Avenue crossed, had been replaced by the figure of a man's face, smoking a huge cigarette. The flowing tip brightened and dulled and streamed from his mouth in imitation of smoke.

A hidden stereopticon threw words on this shifting screen. *Denict cigarettes are safe.*

Wentworth's lips thinned. This widespread death toll, assisted by the diagnosis of doctors, was certainly giving that brand of cigarettes a break. But he had found nothing to connect them with the murders. He glanced at the shops as his taxi toiled slowly through the congested traffic. Windows were placarded in red and green posters, saying also: *Denict cigarettes are safe.* A frown put vertical lines between Wentworth's eyes.

HE STARED at the sidewalks. They were thronged, of course. Not even the dread bony hand of death hovering over them could keep the crowds away from Broadway on this gala night of the year. But somehow the gayety seemed muted. Even the grating of automobile horns seemed dull and flat and the gabble of the shuffling thousands on the walks was full of sibilants as if they could not talk above a whisper.

A street car slammed across the Broadway tracks, plunging into the thick of the Forty-Second street tangle. The metallic clatter was strangely loud. Bawling loudspeakers in front of motion picture theatres were crass and noisy. Wentworth found himself sitting on the edge of his seat, hands gripping the head of his cane tightly.

He glanced up the news bulletin board on the triangular

Times building, letters of light sliding along a narrow strip that girdled the structure.

HOWARD BOISE HAS BEEN NAMED ACTING COMMISSIONER OF POLICE PENDING THE DISCOVERY OF THE WHEREABOUTS OF STANLEY KIRKPATRICK WHO WAS KIDNAPED TODAY FROM HIS FIFTH AVENUE APARTMENT. A $50,000 REWARD....

The roof of the taxi cut off the rest of the sentence. Wentworth nodded grimly as his cab crept around the corner of Forty-Second street. Boise was an energetic and efficient man. He would take the measures that Kirkpatrick should have taken long ago. That was what Wentworth had hoped for. Boise lacked Kirkpatrick's flair for crime detection, but it was better to have an honest plodder in charge than a brilliant madman who was subservient to the murderers.

Wentworth alighted from his cab in front of the glittering entrance of the theatre. Two doors away, a burlesque house flaunted coy nudes in colored life-size lithographs. In front of one sign, three sailors pushed each other about in laughing horse-play.

Wentworth turned toward the Starwyn where the *Delights of 1934* held forth. The show was already on and the outer foyer was nearly deserted. Abruptly, a faint movement in the shadows of a stage entrance alleyway jerked Wentworth's head about. Something was scuttling along the ground, darting across the sidewalk for the gutter—a large gray rat.

As Wentworth watched, a stream of other rodents scampered in its wake, a score, two score of the vermin! For an instant Wentworth stared, feeling the cold slow creep of horror up his spine, feeling the thin tingle of apprehension across his scalp. Twice before now, he had seen animals flee a building and each time it had heralded horrible death. *Poison gas had been loosed in the theatre....*

CHAPTER 14
SPOTLIGHT DEATH

WENTWORTH STOOD rooted to the pavement. A woman cried out in sudden fright, then laughed at her fear as the rats darted into the gutter and disappeared. The three skylarking sailors stared, then laughed boisterously and trooped into the burlesque house. It had been a momentary flurry in the whirlpool of Forty-Second street, but it was already forgotten. The crowd could not know that it heralded wholesale murder.

Wentworth strode rapidly to the corner, his face grimly set. Here was a case in which Boise could act—if he would listen to the Spider. His lips felt stiff as he asked for Boise over the telephone. He moved his tongue dryly in his mouth. He had thought to checkmate the killers for a while with his destruction of the warehouses, and now....

"Boise speaking," the Acting Commissioner's quiet, unhurried voice came over the wire.

Wentworth forced flat, mocking laughter to his lips, made

his voice deep and monotonous, sinister in its lack of accent; the voice that the editor had heard over the wire, the voice that many had come to know as the tones of the dread Spider. Wentworth heard Boise's breath suck in and knew he was recognized.

"The Spider speaking," Wentworth husked. "Those who kill through the smoke men and women breath into their lungs plan to strike tonight at the Starwyn theatre. The gas by which they poison tobacco already has been loosed in the place. If the audience is allowed to smoke in the intermission many will die, horribly. It would be well to confiscate all the tobacco in the place."

"How do you know?" snapped Boise. "What is your part is this infamy?"

Wentworth laughed flatly again. "That fellow, Wentworth, has done the city a good turn in kidnapping Kirkpatrick," he said. "Kirkpatrick would not act. I might duplicate his activity if you don't do better."

"A threat?" Boise was still quiet. It was his self-control which made him dangerous. Anger rarely stirred him. His brain remained clear to function. Wentworth knew that already Boise was attempting to trace this call. It could be done as long as the connection was established.

Once more Wentworth sent his mocking laughter over the wire, then he clicked down the receiver and strolled from the shop. He had deliberately allowed time for the call to be traced. He wanted to spur Boise to action. When Boise learned that the Spider had called from within a half block of the Starwyn, he would certainly come to the theatre. In view of the pending federal action on tobacco, he could scarcely refuse at least to prohibit smoking in the theatre.

Wentworth strolled into the Starwyn. He wore a casual disguise, had paled his complexion and altered his carriage, and made a few subtle changes in the contours of his face. The show was well under way and he waved an alert usher aside, strolled across the back of the theatre, his eyes scanning as much of the audience as he could see, searching the boxes.

Abruptly, he smiled. Deacon Coslin apparently had decided to miss no part of the nudity. He sat in a front box in the second tier and he was leaning forward intently, silhouetted against the stage lights.

The chorus, in spangles and cellophane, was giving him excellent reasons for agitation. There were other shadows of people with him. Wentworth ascended side stairs and made his way quietly toward the box. There was tension in his every movement, a stiffness of muscles that were prepared for any emergency.

He stopped just back of the curtains of the box, peered through the opening. There were three men and two women in Coslin's party. The lawyer, Dewitt Ahearn, the red-headed society woman whom Wentworth had surprised in the cultist's quarters, and Ya Che. The Chinese girl sat remotely in a corner, her attitude relaxed and palpably bored. Her glistening black hair had been plaited and bound about her head in a coronet in which she had set a glittering tiara.

WENTWORTH LOOKED past them to the stage. A long-legged man in evening clothes and silk topper was leaning against the proscenium arch and singing. With a start of his muscles, Wentworth saw that he held a cigarette, lighted, between his fingers. He paused in his singing, waved his cigarette in a nonchalant gesture and touched it to his lips. He sang out smoke. Wentworth half pulled aside the curtain. Ya Che turned slowly and stared up at him, but even while he contemplated interference it was too late. The actor staggered away from the arch, fingers clutching at his throat. His song turned into a hoarse, taut-throated scream. The orchestra's music died discordantly and a dead hush fell over the audience. In that hush the actor screamed again. He was in the middle of the stage now, standing on braced long legs, his head wrenched back between his shoulders. He stared straight upward. His silk hat fell from his head and rolled lopsidedly along the boards.

A woman screamed in the audience, then another. A third began a crazy terrified laughter and men shouted. That sea of white faces became broken, storm-tossed. Men and women surged to their feet. A few stumbled into the aisles and ran for the exits. The actor uttered a third and more horrible scream and blood gushed from his mouth into the orchestra pit. The violence of his nausea threw him down into the shadows where the musicians sat. Wentworth sprang into the box, balanced on the padded outer rail and raised his hands high.

"Spotlight!" he shouted. "Spot—*light!*"

Somewhere up in the misty dark of the theatre's dome, a man caught his cry and, obeying habit, heeded the order. He sent a dazzling white spot light down, picked Wentworth out where he stood on the rim of the theatre box.

141

"You are safe!" Wentworth shouted at the audience. "Safe as long as you don't smoke! Remember the actor smoked! That is what killed him! Stand still! Stand still!"

The white sea of faces twisted toward him. He gestured with his arms, took off his hat.

"Play, maestro!" he called to the orchestra.

"You are safe," he cried again. "Safe as long as you don't smoke! Throw away your cigars and cigarettes!"

The shouting and turmoil below was quieting. Somewhere a woman still laughed and sobbed in hysteria. House lights began to spring and a faint first strain of music whimpered from the violins in the orchestra.

A bull roar behind Wentworth made him whirl. Coslin was on his feet, head down. He was plunging toward Wentworth his arms thrust out full length to knock him from his precarious perch and hurl him down among the audience.

"The Spider!" he gasped hoarsely. "The Spider! I know your voice, and…."

He stumbled over a chair, thrust mightily at Wentworth's legs. But Wentworth was not there. With a slight tensing of his legs, he slapped both hands upon Deacon Coslin's head and vaulted clean over him. Coslin stumbled to his knees, striking his forehead against the rail. Wentworth sprang to the curtains, found them whipped aside, saw Ya Che's round white arm holding them back and leaped past, whirling down a steep flight of stairs.

He heard the sharp rap of high heels behind him, turned his head.

142

"Wait!" Ya Che sent her soft, deep voice after him. "Wait and save me!"

She overtook him with a stuttering little run, her trailing brocade gown drawn high to clear her ankles. Her hand closed upon his arm and her deep, lightless eyes turned upward to his.

"You alone can save me," she said.

WENTWORTH HESITATED a moment. He suspected that she and her father were tied up with one or the other of the two gangs of Chinese that were spreading death and destruction over the land. She might well be leading him into a trap. But he was already in a trap. Police must be in the building to forestall the slaughter he had warned about. They would have heard Coslin's cry. Abruptly, Wentworth laughed. There was a way out.

He stooped and picked up Ya Che, an arm beneath her knees, the other holding her shoulders.

"You have fainted, Ya Che," he told her softly, "let your arms and your head hang."

Ya Che ran a swift hand up to her head and loosened the glorious black veil of her hair. With a slow smile into Wentworth's eyes, she slipped a strap of her dress over her shoulder. Her décolletage was very low and the swelling curve of her breast was disclosed as she allowed her head and arm to sag. She relaxed against Wentworth's chest.

With a grim smile in his eyes, but with stiff fright on his face, Wentworth strode toward the front door of the theatre. Ya Che had played her cards well. No one would look at the Spider while he carried so gorgeously disheveled a burden. He reached the lobby. A line of blue coated policemen stood guard there.

143

"She must have air," Wentworth said hurriedly. "Fainted."

The policeman toward whom Wentworth pushed looked not at Wentworth, but at the down-hanging head of the girl, at her long black hair that reached nearly to the ground and at her ivory-smooth shoulder. He sucked in his breath.

"Man, oh, man!" he murmured and stepped aside.

Wentworth went past him swiftly, shouldered open the door and strode to the curb. Instantly, a long-nosed car slid from the parking ranks and a uniformed Chinese leaped from the box to open the door. His face was utterly impassive but there was a glitter in his eyes. For an instant, Wentworth hesitated. Death might well lurk there in the dark depths of the car. His hands were useless now, holding Ya Che. With a low whine of siren, a black police phaeton squealed brakes at the curb and Wentworth saw the white, set face of Howard Boise as the man climbed from its rear seat.

With a tightening of his lips; he bowed his head and climbed into Ya Che's car. He lifted her body high before him as a shield and her hair brushed his cheek. A faint perfume was warm in his nostrils. Her eyes were half open and a faint smile curved the pale softness of her lips.

Then they were inside and Wentworth saw that his fears had been unfounded. If the attack was coming, it would be later. Save for themselves, the car was empty. He set Ya Che down upon the cushions and the sedan surged forward. He straightened, easing his arms from under the girl and she lifted her head slowly, that enigmatic smile still upon her lips. She did not put up her hair; she did not draw the shoulder strap into place.

"Is it that you are afraid of me... Spider?" she asked softly, and Wentworth caught the faint deep slurring of her voice, the almost indefinable accent. The car had wormed through the traffic of Forty-second Street and was swinging south on Eighth Avenue. Store fronts and street lights filtered a dim, flickering illumination into the tonneau where they sat.

"Terribly afraid," Wentworth said softly. He leaned toward her so that his eyes were not far from hers, so that the warm fragrance of her breath fanned his mouth. His lips, too, were smiling. "Terribly afraid," he repeated and there was mockery in his voice. Ya Che ignored that. She leaned toward him—but it was scarcely that. No more than a slight movement of that warm bared shoulder, a dropping of her eyelids.

"Oh what?" she asked. Her pale mouth barely framed the words, and they left her lips parted.

WENTWORTH MOVED forward, too, so that there was no more than an inch between their lips, so that the fragrance that was in her hair, and the smell of her was in his nostrils. For a long moment they stayed like that, half-closed eyes of blue-gray gazing deep into the dead black of her heavy-lidded gaze. Then he kissed her, but without feeling, a light half-humorous peck such as a man might give a child. Even so, her shoulders shuddered toward him, her breath sucked in, her eyes closed. Wentworth drew back and, from his corner, laughed lightly. "Terribly afraid," he said again and his dry tones were a mockery.

Ya Che sat bolt upright. He caught a dull gleam in her eyes that was like light on dull gray murderous steel. She drew the shoulder strap into place and began to plait her hair with calm, slow-moving hands. Her voice when it came was placid, even slightly amused.

"I always said you were… old enough, Spider," she said.

Wentworth's face was bantering, but he knew that there was a slow heavy throbbing in his chest, that the palms of his hands were moist. This woman had secrets that might save a nation. Of that he was positive. If she were handled properly, he might learn those secrets. But the way did not lie in instantaneous capitulation to her allure. Whatever trap she prepared for him must not find him with sensuously drugged mind. He must be alert and ready.

Yet his heart pounded against his ribs, and he knew that though he had mocked her, he was… terribly afraid. The woman was like a gorgeous snake. There was a fascination in the dead black beauty of her eyes, a fascination that would draw a man down and down into the gulf she prepared for him. There was something deadly there, too—something that repelled shudderingly in the same instant that her allure was greatest. Her lips would be warm.

"You said I could save you," he said calmly and his voice gave no indication of his stress.

He saw the woman's head nod against the passing lights. "Those blackmailers who threatened Dewitt Ahearn," she said. "They have warned me. At midnight they say they will strike, unless we pay." Her voice grew brittle with scorn. "As if the Wu paid tribute to scum!"

"At midnight?" Wentworth" queried softly. He held up his

watch dial and read the greenish glimmer of its radium-painted figures. "An hour yet"

"We will need most of that to reach my home," she said.

She sat relaxed in her corner now, slim long hands folded in her lap. No one would have guessed that moments ago, her lips… Wentworth drove the thought from his mind. Twice this day, he had defeated the plans of the dread killer, but as yet he was no nearer the elimination of the fiend than at the start of the battle. And the man had taken heavy toil in return.

Wentworth moved restlessly in his seat. The car had writhed across the city now and was trundling down the East Side. It stopped in front of a rich mansion in the Gramercy section and the liveried Chinese jumped down from the box to swing the door wide. Wentworth alighted with a hand for Ya Che's arm. She had drawn a fur-lined wrap about her shoulders now, the frosty white of its collar like snow against the black night of her hair. Together they moved across the walk. The door was swung wide by another Chinese.

Ya Che's voice, sharp with command, addressed the man and he bowed low, hands hidden in voluminous sleeves, opened broad doors to the left, disappeared. Then a quavering, high-pitched cry seared the air. Wentworth passed Ya Che in a bound, saw the Chinese standing with hands flung high in an open doorway. He darted to the man's side, hand on his gun.

As he reached the servant, the man thunder-bolted backward, sending Wentworth spinning before he could dodge. He had a confused glimpse of the room beyond, a small study whose walls were lined with books, of a tottering old Chinese upon whose chin tufted the five-strand beard of venerable wisdom. He was clutching at his throat, screaming terribly. It was Wu Chang. Two men were plunging out of the study. The knife of one had struck deep into the servant's chest, the force of the blow hurling him back upon Wentworth. Both had guns in their hands. They blasted as Wentworth tripped over a rumpled rug and went down with the corpse, of the Chinese servant spilling across him, pinning his gun hand to his chest. The whole scene was a storm....

CHAPTER 15
THE CRIMSON VEIL AGAIN

WENTWORTH REALIZED two things sharply, even in the brief moment while he plunged to the floor. Wu Chang, the man whom above all others he had suspected of implication in the wholesale murders that were sweeping the country, had been murdered—murdered by the strangling hands of the gas. Also he and Ya Che had seen the faces of the killers and their lives were forfeit. But for the moment this body that pinned his gun hand to his chest, shielded him from bullets.

He heard Ya Che's voice rip out in piercing, scathing Chinese. The tones themselves were blistering. He heard a light automatic crack, then the heavier boom of assassin's guns. With a wrench, Wentworth tossed aside the body that imprisoned him, flung to his knees and snapped his gun clear. The two men were plunging toward the doorway. He glimpsed the flash of Ya Che's silvery gown as she dodged inside a room across the hall, saw a spurt of flame from her hand as she whirled at bay.

Wentworth fired deliberately at the man nearest the door and the lead clubbed the killer to his knees, pitched him prone at Ya Che's feet. The second killer whirled around the doorjamb, thrust back his hand and emptied a forty-four automatic in a continuous roll of gunfire, spraying lead wildly across the room. Flat on his belly, Wentworth fired once more and his bullet smashed through the hand, sent the automatic slamming against the wall. With a screech of pain, the man fled.

In three bounds, Wentworth was in the hall. Ya Che swung out from hiding with her automatic ready, her face twisted with rage. Wentworth swept down the barrel of his weapon and smacked the pistol from her hand. The fleeing assassin ripped open the door and raced out into the night with his right arm dangling, and Ya Che whirled on Wentworth with her long nails clawing for his face.

With a stiff-armed thrust he hurled her back against the wall, pinned her there with thumb and fingers gripping her throat. "Two lives cannot avenge your father," he snapped. "Let that one live so we can follow him to his master."

Ya Che jerked a dagger from the throat of her dress and lifted it. Then, even while Wentworth jerked up his automatic to parry it, she checked the blow. Wentworth's words had been slow in penetrating her anger. Her breath was hissing through bared white teeth, her breasts jerked with the panting of her anger. She nodded her head, fought articulate words through the rage.

"Right," she got out. "You are right. Let us follow!"

Wentworth snatched his hand from her throat and reached the door with long strides, hurled out into the street. It was a narrow street, smooth-paved, with small graceful trees spaced along its length. At the eastern end, it ran into a small fenced park and the roadway detoured to left and right. For a moment the street seemed empty, then Wentworth spotted a moving shadow close against the opposite line of houses. He darted out into the night with Ya Che at his heels. She had snatched up only her fur-lined cloak and she dragged that in one hand, ignoring the bite of the cold that was still and bitter in the street.

Together they ran after the fleeing figure and the man staggered out from the wall and sprinted. He flashed around the corner and an automobile motor roared into life, the car spurted across the street's end and the whine of rubber as it swung about the right angle curves of the park floated back. Wentworth missed Ya Che beside him, but ran on. This was a wealthy neighborhood and there should be plenty of taxis about.

He reached the corner, stood and peered swiftly about, whistled shrilly on his fingers. A motor muttered down the street he had left, he heard Ya Che's clear call and spun to find that the car which had brought them from the theatre was sliding to a halt beside him. He sprang in.

"The car went straight east," he snapped.

The forward surge of the car slammed him back on the cushions. He pushed himself erect, and peered ahead as tires moaned in the swing about the tiny square. When they reached the street on the opposite side, the way ahead was dark and deserted.

"South!" Wentworth snapped.

THE CHINESE driver spun the wheel, the motor throbbed and its rhythm rose to a moan. The man was small, the wheel seeming too large for his narrow-shouldered bulk, but he handled the long-nosed machine masterfully.

"East, then south again," Wentworth ordered.

They swung like that, two whistling, lurching skids with scarcely diminished speed. Three blocks ahead, a tail-light bobbed in frantic flight. The car dived through a white pool of street light. Wentworth uttered a little exclamation of triumph.

"That's the car," he barked. "Don't overtake it, but don't lose it either!"

He settled back into the cushions. Ya Che's voice, in mono-syllabic Chinese, spat out words. The driver hunched forward over his wheel and there was a cringe in the way his head thrust out. The woman settled back into the cushions, too.

Wentworth guessed she had added a threat of some kind to make sure the chauffeur did not lose the trail. She was breathing deeply and slowly through her nose and the respirations were audible. She still clutched the light automatic, snatched from the floor where Wentworth had knocked it. The dagger had disappeared.

Wentworth looked at her with a new estimate of her character. He had known she would be dangerous, but he had scarcely expected such smooth and instant fighting capacity. Her shot had gone wild, apparently, but her bravery and her strategy had been unquestionable. She had darted to cover and opened fire. His intervention was the one thing that had saved the life of the man they now pursued. Rage had distorted her face, but now it

was utterly calm, her eyes inscrutable beneath heavy lids. Only
her disturbed breathing, the rapid rise and fall of her breasts,
betrayed her emotion and even that was quieting rapidly. Yet
back there in that quiet home, her father lay dead upon the floor,
victim of the pernicious poison that the murderous Chinese had
planted for him.

Wentworth peered ahead again, saw that they were still on

the trail of the fugitive and began to build again his ideas of the case. He had centered all his beliefs ultimately on the idea that Wu Chang, pilgrim of venerable wisdom, actually was the brain behind all these infamies. Now that structure crumpled and crashed with the murder of that man, apparently by the hirelings of the Master Killer himself.

There had been no time to examine the body of the man his

The two cars met head-on at almost equal speed.

lead had killed, but Wentworth knew they had used the tobacco poison. That was proof enough. He smiled tensely. Somewhere ahead on this trail tonight he would contact the real terrorist the Red Mandarin. When they did… Wentworth found he was leaning forward, clutching the grip of his automatic in a tense grip. Yes, it would come like that, swift lead to wipe out this menace to America.

Suddenly as death itself, a black car shot from a side street ramming straight for their sedan! Wentworth's cry of warning and the swift shriek in Chinese of Ya Che were as one word. The little driver ahead seemed to stand erect in a wrench upon the wheel. He whirled, not away from the charging car, but directly to meet its attack.

There was an instant of shrieking rubber as the tires bit against the pavement, a momentary belch of gun shots from the other car. Ya Che's car had been traveling more swiftly, but the turn had slowed it. The two would meet with almost equal speed. Wentworth had just time to brace his feet against the partition ahead of him, to throw his left arm in front of Ya Che, when the ramming shock of the cars meeting nose-on bent him double. He glimpsed the surging rise of the driver's body as the suddenly arrested momentum of the machine launched him head first through his windshield, taking the steering wheel with him.

WENTWORTH'S HEAD bumped his own braced legs, knocked them loose from their hold, smacked him down on the floor of the car. Ya Che spilled down on top of him. The crash and tinkle of glass, the grinding of metal on metal was deafening. The motor of the sedan still raced, the tires urging it forward upon the wreck of the other machine.

Frightened shouts rang out. The killers had not expected that swift, ramming swirl of Ya Che's car. They had expected to ram broadside, back off with no more than a bent fender and smashed headlights and finish their prey with gunfire.

Wentworth fought out from under the burden of Ya Che's weight upon his shoulders, fought off the dazing numbness of the shock and pushed the door open.

He reeled out on the street with gun in hand. Still unsteady on his feet, he lunged toward the other car. The driver was crumpled forward over the wheel, inert and motionless. Ya Che's driver had been hurled like a projectile and his broken body lay suddenly on the roof of the gangster car, legs dangling down on the hood. The dazzling glare of a single overhead street light blazed down upon them, glistened on black blood that dripped, dripped from the gangster car.

Wentworth reached the machine, wrenched open the back door. A man raised himself weakly from the floor. There was a glint of metal, but Wentworth's gun blasted first. He saw the man's face in the lurid glare of his powder flame—saw it vanish in a spatter of blood from his soft-nosed slug. But the glimpse had been enough. The man was Chinese. Windows were flinging up in the tenements now. Heads and shoulders showed against yellow light. Shouts and queries—excited gabble—filled the street. A police whistle bit through the night.

Wentworth flashed a light upon the interior of the car. One of the four men in the car was moving feebly, one on the back

155

seat. Wentworth seized him by the collar and hauled him clear. He jammed his gun against the man's eye.

"Where are your headquarters?" he snarled. "Quick, fool! Death is here."

A glimmer of steel thrust past him, the point of Ya Che's dagger touched the man's throat. Chinese spat from Ya Che's lips. The man's eyes rolled, his head strained upward, stretched his yellow throat taut against the prick of the dagger. A stream of words bubbled from his mouth. An exclamation of triumph burst from Ya Che. She thrust the dagger home, hilt deep in the man's throat.

"Come," she told Wentworth sharply. "It is not far."

Wentworth let the man sag to the ground, tossing his body dear so that the quick spurting blood would not soil him. His lips were tight and there was a steely gleam to his eyes. He had killed, yes, but he did not kill like this, murdering a helpless man as this strange calm woman did. He spun and seized her wrist, twisted the dagger from her hand, took the automatic

"I'll keep these," he said coldly. "Lead on."

Ya Che reeled back against the wrecked car with the vehemence of his action. Her face was dead calm, but once more there was the dull gleam in her eyes as if on the gray deadly point of a sword. Slowly she drew about her throat the collar of her fur-lined cloak and the whiteness strengthened the inky black of her hair, the ivory pallor of her face. Her lips curved slightly and the smile was scornful.

"Come," she said.

She circled the automobiles so that they were between them

156

and the slapping feet, the trilling whistle that marked the approach of the policeman. They reached the shadows, skirted a tenement to reach an alley and turned into that. The woman's clothing was a ghostly gleam in the darkness and the dim aroma of her hair touched his nostrils. Wentworth's nose thinned. That perfume should be redolent of spilled blood, but it was sensuous, still alluring. Before this, he had met women who killed with a smile, who could torture fiendishly. But there had been something warped and horrible about them. This woman was utterly calm. Her ferocity sprang from a basic disregard for human life, from racial cruelty.

"These headquarters," Wentworth asked, "where are they?"

"Two blocks along this alley," Ya Che told him calmly. "The third house from the corner and the entrance is through the cellar."

WENTWORTH NODDED in the darkness, but said nothing. He wondered if the Chinese had given more detailed instructions for entrance, but realized that he had spoken too briefly for that. They came out on a cross street and moved toward the dimness of the alley again. Three doors beyond the next corner... Wentworth glanced right and left, spotted the black bulge of a police box fastened to a house wall.

"Wait," he snapped at Ya Che and raced to the box. A single blow of his gun smashed the lock. He jerked it open and rang. Ya Che reached his side as he shouted a swift alarm into the mouthpiece. She reached for the cutoff, but Wentworth held her at arm's length until he had finished.

"You fool!" Ya Che snapped at him. "The police will be here before we can get into the place."

"Probably," Wentworth agreed. He did not explain, but he knew the odds against his own successful conquest of the headquarters of the gang were remote. By the time they reached there, the wounded killer would have arrived, warned that he was pursued. They would not know, of course, the result of the attack by the other car, but if they did not, on the heels of his arrival, receive assurances of success, they would know that failure had attended the attempt.

At any rate, they would be warned and he and Ya Che were entering the building without detailed knowledge of the way of approach. It might well be that the police would come only in time to save the Spider's life. It would be instantly forfeit, of course, but he would take his chances on escaping from their imprisonment, rather than from the guns of the gang. He must be inside when they struck, to make sure that the leader died....

They reached the third house and Ya Che slipped from him and swung open, soundlessly, a section of the fence. He followed; saw the frosty white of her fur as a dim luminousness in the dark. He trailed her along the length of the yard. Ya Che seemed to see her way with the facility of a cat. They crossed the cellar, pushed up stairs and Wentworth took the lead, listening at a door.

Beyond it was no sound at all.

"My gun," Ya Che requested with calm firmness.

Wentworth hesitated, then shrugged and yielded not only the gun, but the knife. If he failed, if the gangsters knocked him down, she would have need of both to survive until the arrival of the police. He turned the knob silently, thrust the door open quietly and stepped into a room. Ya Che was close behind him.

Abruptly the door clapped shut. Lights blazed on and Wentworth looked into the steady muzzles of guns in the hands of four grim hoods. There were two other men in the room. One was lying on the floor dead, his right hand shattered. Wentworth recognized him as the man his bullet had winged in Wu Chang's house. The sixth man wore a crimson mask that dangled from the inner edge of his hat, a mask which was a veil through which nothing was visible, but through which the killer could see. And he was tall and thin as a skeleton in clothes!

"Welcome to this unworthy domicile," the gaunt man said with a sibilant accent that was mocking and unhurried. "It is unfortunate, but this humble one must insist that you remain—forever.'"

He lifted a hand casually, a signal to the killers to strike. Wentworth swept Ya Che from her feet with a thrust of his arm. His gun spat upward twice, blasting out the lights. He sprang straight through the darkness.

His gun racketed twice more; then the sword of a flashlight stabbed through the thick darkness of the room. He saw that one man was down, writhing, and he sped two more bullets into the blackness behind the fan of the light.

A scream rewarded him. Then his charge smashed into a man and he slashed upward with his pistol barrel. The blow was blocked short, catching on an arm, and his encircling left arm found that he had grappled with the veiled leader. No other man could be so bonily tall, so powerful in that instant of contact. His lips bared his teeth.

"I have him," the man's voice rang out. "Come and kill him!"

WENTWORTH SMASHED again with his automatic muzzle; then a blow crunched on his head. He reeled backward, saw blazing lights come into the room again. He found abruptly that he was on the floor, that the tall man with the crimson veil was crouched forward, gripping a blackjack. That was what had felled Wentworth. The man raised the blackjack again and Wentworth heard behind him the spiteful small bark of Ya Che's weapon, heard harsh voices shouting.

Wentworth's automatic was still in his hand and one shot remained in it. He strained his muscles to lift that hand, but it was incredibly heavy. He threw every atom of will into the effort, felt the gun come clear of the floor. The crimson veil swayed toward him and from under it bubbled a queer sound. He realized that the leader was laughing, that he was toying with him, the blackjack ready to smack him into oblivion the instant he raised the pistol a little higher....

Ya Che was screaming curses behind him. The light gun barked again. Wentworth waited, the gun half-raised, gathering strength and will power. Abruptly he pulled up the muzzle. With a curse, the man in the crimson veil slashed down. A terrific crash deafened Wentworth. Was it his gun, or was it the blackjack smacking against his skull? Lights blazed intolerably bright before him. They flashed and faded. The darkness of unconsciousness was black... and bottomless....

CHAPTER 16
THE RED MANDARIN

THERE WAS a fuzziness about Wentworth's brain that refused to lift—a damp gray cloud of inertia that weighed him like leaden shoes. Now and then, a soft voice penetrated to his consciousness; sometimes stabbing pain made him writhe. Finally things became clear about him. He was in bed. The room was luxurious in the extreme. A Chinese sat beside him.

Wentworth rolled his head and the Chinese rose to his feet and left the room. The door opened again and Ya Che entered. She wore crimson pajamas with a long jacket that came almost to her knees and their embroidery was in gold thread. The burning flame would have bleached most women to pale insignificance, but Ya Che dominated it, made the crimson enhance her own dark beauty.

She glided to his bedside, "I am glad," she said quietly.

Wentworth tried to speak and his throat felt rusty. He tried again and succeeded. "What day is this?" he demanded. "What happened?"

"This is the twenty-ninth of December," she said calmly. "You killed three men and I killed two. We hid until the police had left. It was a long time and I thought you would die."

"I killed... three men?" His eyes repeated the question.

Ya Che nodded. "You killed the man with the crimson veil," she said. "He was a very inferior person by the name of Hsa Tze."

A frown made Wentworth's head throb with pain. Hsa Tze

161

meant fool. A peculiar name even for a Chinese. He lifted a hand slowly and felt thick bandages about his skull.

"A fracture," Ya Che said. "It will be long before you can move again."

Long? But it could not be long, it must not be. He... The gray mist swirled in his brain again and he slept. When he awoke again, he lay with his eyes closed. He was aware of a subtle fragrance, a scent that he recognized. Ya Che. But he heard nothing. She must be sitting quietly beside him. He opened his eyes, looked about. Ya Che was seated beside him and, meeting his eyes, she smiled faintly.

"I must tell you today," she said. "I can see that you are ready. We are prisoners of the Red Mandarin. I did not tell you the whole truth yesterday."

Wentworth's eyes met the woman's without change of expression, but the thing she had said struck into his mind like fiery pain. Killing the man of the Crimson Veil had accomplished nothing then. The menace that had threatened America still hung over the heads of the people. He had slain, but the killings had been futile—and he was helpless in the hands of the Master himself. But, if that were so, why was he still alive? As if she sensed that query, Ya Che answered: "We are alive because I persuaded the Mandarin that we two would be useful to him. He was inclined to be merciful because you had wiped out a man who worked against him, who aped his manners and personality and used them for personal gain. That pleased him. This afternoon, in a few hours, you are to go before the Mandarin.

I beg you to think well before you make the decision he will require of you."

Wentworth closed his eyes again. Every effort at thought brought the swirling mists of unconsciousness close to him again. But was it unconsciousness? Rather it was a deep lethargy, an inertia that made even the effort to think a terrific burden. His will seemed a limp and useless thing. But in the depths of his mind something that would not yield was stirring. That something cried to him to fight.

HE LOOKED at Ya Che again. Her eyes were opened wide, their dull black depths like pools of restfulness. They invited him to plunge deep into them and rest, rest... Wentworth closed his eyes again and that spark in the back of his mind burned higher. Now it signaled not fight, but *danger*.

"I'm tired," Wentworth murmured. "Let me sleep."

A small sound of satisfaction came from Ya Che. He heard the rustle of silk as she stood. "Sleep, weary one," she said softly. "I think that when we face the Red Mandarin, you will decide... as you should decide."

Wentworth said nothing. He made his breathing deep and regular and heard the door close. He kept his eyes shut then and continued his deception while he battled against the weary weakness that told him nothing was worthwhile; that it was better to sleep than to think; that it would be simpler to do what the Red Mandarin would presently ask than to fight. And in the back of his brain, that small spark that was Richard Wentworth's inner self flamed higher and higher. Its message was fight, *fight*, FIGHT....

163

This was the monster behind
the thousands of murders which
had swept the nation.

Lying flat on his back, motionless and with closed eyes, Wentworth fought the greatest battle of his career, fought back the gray mists of numbness, fought for coherent thought. Sweat popped out on his forehead, throbbing pain stabbed through his brain, his fingers clenched until the muscles of his forearms ached… In the end he slept.

A touch on his forehead awoke him and he struggled erect, weak and pale, and with the assistance of a Chinese servant got into clothing. His eyes were heavy-lidded and dull, his steps dragging when finally, assisted by two men, he moved behind Ya Che down a dim corridor and into a great room whose walls were draped with black satin.

The lights in this room were faint, too, and they were all red. Their luminance rose and fell like the glow of coals that a gusty wind breathes on. The gleam made snakes of red upon the satin of the walls.

Beneath Wentworth's stumbling feet, the carpet was deep and soundless and that, too, was solid black. He raised his heavy head, and looking across the room, saw that they approached a blood-colored throne. Upon it, a man draped from head to foot in robes of scarlet silk was sitting. From a black mitered cap hung a scarlet veil that completely concealed the man's face. A giant Negro stood on his right and a giant from northern China on his left. Their torsos were bare except for a loin cloth of scarlet. The fluctuating glow from the braziers cast a ruddy light upon their bodies. Arms folded, each man grasped in his right hand a bare curved sword with a heavy blade that was fully four feet long.

As the full significance of the scene pierced Wentworth's mind, he stopped in the center of the black room and stared. This was the Master behind the thousands of murders that had swept the nation, laying it bleeding and helpless at this man's feet. This was the monster who had struck at him through Nita, through Kirkpatrick, through the machinations of scores of slavish henchmen. This was the schemer who held his life now in the palm of his hand who had a proposition to make to the Spider.

The hands that gripped Wentworth's arms thrust forward again and his head sagged, he moved on sluggish feet to the throne. The men to his right and left dropped to their knees, touched their foreheads to the floor And Wentworth—the Spider who had defied a hundred master-minds of crime, who had sworn undying enmity to all things evil—Wentworth also dropped on his knees and *bent his head to the floor!*

THE RED MANDARIN tensed on his throne as if he, too, were amazed that this Master of Men should bow before him. Ya Che was standing straight and tall, her eyes focused on the veil that covered the man's face.

"You may rise," the Mandarin said in sibilant English. In his tones was gloating—gloating over his foe who had fallen so low. Wentworth got cumbersomely to his feet. The faces of the two guards were sneering.

"O man who call yourself after the spider," the Mandarin chanted. "I am inclined to be lenient with you. You removed a foe who was loathsome to me and you come humbly for mercy..." He paused as if expecting some denial there, but Wentworth only swayed woodenly on his feet, half-closed eyes raised no higher than the knees of the Red Mandarin. "I have decided to grant that mercy, if you will do as I direct."

Wentworth moved his right hand in a small, resigned gesture. It was as if he said this was the end of the battle, that what this man ordered, he would do. His bandaged head seemed too heavy to raise.

"There are certain leaders," the Mandarin went on slowly, "whom even my men cannot reach. Yet they are men who must be controlled—or removed—if my plans are to succeed. I cannot touch them, I admit, but you, O Spider...."

He leaned forward. Through that red veil, his evil eyes were peering. Their gleam almost seemed to shine through the crimson cloth, the cloth that masked the identity of this mad killer.

"If you will agree to remove these men, O Spider," the Mandarin hissed, "then not only shall you live, but you shall share in my triumph. And it will be mighty. The gold shall fall into your lap like ripe figs. There shall be... women..." The red veiled face swung toward the impassive countenance of Ya Che, toward her dead black eyes staring still straight ahead. "Or if you wish, in the silly manner of your race, to cling only to one woman...."

Wentworth's head came up slowly. His eyes were hidden behind the droop of his lids, but an electric thrill of tension raced through his body. Could that possibly mean Nita? But the effort of thinking was too great. His head sagged down again.

"One woman," the Mandarin repeated, and there was regret in his voice. "I shall return to you the one you love."

He lifted his right hand slightly from the scarlet arm of the scarlet throne and, with a whispering swish of silk, the curtains on his left swept back.

"Look, Spider!" the Mandarin commanded.

Slowly Wentworth's head came up again, heavily swung toward the parted curtains. A shudder swept over him. Beyond that curtain were two small alcoves whose fronts were steel bars. Soft yellow light flooded those cells. In one, a huge furry animal squatted like a man on the floor. It lifted its head and evil red eyes gleamed; lips snarled back from yellow fangs. The beast straightened, rising to its feet so that it stood with hunched formidable shoulders. Arboreal hands clutched the bars and the fearful strength of the thing made them shake.

"An orangutan," the Mandarin explained softly. "He is easily as powerful as the gorilla and much more human. For instance, they have been known to seize and carry off native women. The women die ultimately, of course, but in the meantime…."

WENTWORTH'S DULL eyes had opened wide with incredulous staring. In the other cell was—Good God! *It was Nita!*

Nita was standing, gripping the bars also. Her lovely body was nearly nude, clad in the filmy garments of a woman of the *Seraglio.* Upon her body, a little jacket that was open its full length barely covered her exquisite breasts. Low on her hips was a girdle with a jeweled clasp and from it depended a silken skirt of such extraordinary weave that it scarcely seemed to exist. It enhanced the subtle curve of her hips, glorified the shapely white columns of her limbs. The glorious chestnut hair hung to her shoulders, and the yellow lights made fiery gleams among its curls. But on her face was such a mingling of joy and pain as would tear the heart. Her red lips were tremulous. She reached supplicant hands between the bars, her warm round arms petitioning.

"Dick! Oh, Dick!" she cried. "You, too!"

Wentworth took two stumbling steps toward her, his hands trembling as he stretched them forward. The black silken curtains swished down again, swirled together and the yellow light was blotted. Wentworth went on, two, three, four faltering steps. His hands touched the curtains and he whipped them aside sluggishly. A black wall was before him, a black wall that rang dully with the clangor of steel as he beat his fits against it.

"Nita! Nita!" he cried.

Only the sibilant laughter of the Red Mandarin answered him. He whirled about, his shoulders against that steel wall, staring toward the scarlet throne.

"She shall be yours, O Spider," the Red Mandarin said. "And she is unharmed. I'll concede that she has been a temptation, but she is unharmed, for I anticipated this day. Yours, O Spider, if you assent...."

He hesitated and Wentworth felt the skin tighten behind his ears, felt muscles bunch along his jaws, the tightening of his lips that lifted them from his teeth. There was something in this man that evoked the primitive within him, that stirred red animal rage. It was on Wentworth's face now, for the two guards, the Chinese and the Negro unfolded their arms and the great four-foot blades gleamed red as though with blood in the brazier light as they pointed toward Wentworth.

But Wentworth's shoulder did not leave the steel wall. Something horrible was brewing here, something beyond the imagination of white men. Behind that crimson mask that hid God alone knew what evil, there was a hissing, whistle sound that might have been amusement, that might have been the greedy lip-sucking of some unimaginable beast.

"If you do not assent, O Spider," his sing-song, emotionless voice spoke on, "you shall be a witness to something that scientists the world over have longed to see and have not dared—perhaps have lacked the courage to witness."

He paused again and once more the whistling, hissing laughter that could scarcely be called laughter seeped out from behind that mask.

Wentworth's chest jerked with spasmodic breathing, his fists knotted until the muscles writhed in his arms.

The Mandarin continued: "The orangutan has been waiting eagerly ever since Kirkpatrick was kind enough to send Nita into our trap."

KIRKPATRICK HAD betrayed Nita into his hands? The thought did not register in Wentworth's mind. He recorded it, but his brain was wholly occupied with hate and fear. His eyes did not swerve from the veil that swathed the Red Mandarin's face. With a hoarse cry, he propelled himself from his stand against the wall, charging blindly for the Mandarin despite those powerful guards and their four-foot swords—despite the hundred servitors who must crouch behind these walls.

"Don't kill him," the Mandarin said softly.

The two guards stepped forward, lithe muscles cording beneath their bare skins. One seized Wentworth's arm on each side. He squirmed and fought, but it was useless. He was weak from illness. A kind of terrible calmness came to Wentworth—a calmness that sat like a demon in his brain while his body still struggled against the strength of these two giants. That calmness seemed to detach his soul from his body so that he stood aloof and watched himself writhe in the grip of those two men. Finally he ceased the battle.

"Yes, my dear Spider," intoned the Mandarin. "You shall be a witness to a marvelous spectacle; you shall be as helpless as you are now to interfere. I hope that you will treasure the little treat I have in store for you—if you do not agree to my plans."

Wentworth was gulping the hot-scented air of the room with great panting gasps. He stood rigid with a giant's hand clamped to each arm. He fought for the calmness with which hitherto he had faced such emergencies. It was not the first time that criminals battling him had struck at his integrity through Nita. They had captured her and threatened death by hanging, by torture. They had threatened to make her a dope addict and turn her into a woman of the streets by that insidious method. And he had defied them all, had fought down the fierce love within him and refused to bow to criminal demands even if he meant that he himself should be put upon the rack of heart-torture forever, even if it meant that Nita, his darling Nita, should suffer untold agonies of body and soul.

For it had been only upon this basis that he and Nita had allowed themselves the solace of their love. Wentworth had known that he had no right to love when he had pledged himself to the eternal service of humanity, to ceaseless battle against the underworld. But their love had been too great. It had hurdled even that obstacle. And Wentworth and Nita had pledged themselves that not all hell should swerve them from the stern path of duty, even should the one they loved be torn to pieces before his eyes.

They had pledged that, and up until now, Wentworth had clung rigidly to that course of action. Time and again, he had defied the underworld until he had believed that his integrity was established, until he was sure that the vast grapevine that carries the intelligences of the underworld had spread everywhere the fact that the Spider could not be reached through his love. Yet here was a man who had ignored that, a man who knew the deep primitive psychology of man's heart and could play upon it as a minstrel plucks his harp. He knew that a man might mentally consent to the death of a loved one in the interests of inexorable duty, but he knew, too, that a man compelled to witness that sacrifice might weaken in his mental pledge when torn by the dictates of his heart. He only need make the sacrifice horrible enough....

"I must have time to think," Wentworth said and his voice was a hoarse croak that startled even his own ears. "Time to think. First, I must know whose life it is that you wish sacrificed. And I must regain my strength. As it is now, I would be seized by the first policeman I passed on the street."

TIME, *time!* He must have time. If he could only think. There might be some way out. He was here in the stronghold of the monster; it was true, surrounded by his servants, facing death on every hand. Nita was here, too, and he knew there was no chance of escape. Stubbornly he clung to hope.

"You shall have time," the Mandarin said, and Wentworth's chest rose in an inhalation of hope, but the Mandarin leaned forward and once more Wentworth fancied a fiend's eyes gleamed even through that veil of silk. "You shall have time, but first I want your pledge to help. I know that once the Spider gives his word, he does not go back upon it. Afterwards, you shall have as much time as you wish to regain your strength."

Once more Wentworth felt a surge of primitive rage, felt his lips snarl back from his teeth. He was conscious of the tightening grip upon his arms, heard the quick breath of Ya Che at his elbow. The Mandarin was tensed forward. The jade-guarded nails of his hands seemed to tremble slightly. Wentworth forced the snarl from his lips, forced them into a faint, stiff smile.

"I advise you not to compel an answer at once," he said clearly.

"You advise!" The Mandarin's voice shrilled. Rage thinned it "*You* advise. You will obey when I speak!"

Wentworth's stiff smile became tighter. "I am the Spider," he said slowly. "Men know that I do not speak lightly. I tell you that if you compel me to decide now, the answer will be—" He drew himself up slightly, his head flung back, eyes meeting the Mandarin's hidden gaze. That small action seemed to increase the tension of the room, tightened the breath of those who watched. His voice rang out clearly. "The answer will be *no!*"

For a full two minutes after he ceased speaking, there was complete silence in the room, a silence that swelled into audible ringing waves of rhythm, a silence that was unbroken save for

the hurried breathing of Ya Che, save for the beating of Wentworth's heart that seemed to rise within his brain like savage
tom-toms, heralding death. Abruptly the Mandarin hissed out a
word like a curse. His right hand lifted and once more there was
a swishing swirl of silk as the curtains bared the cells where Nita
and that fearful beast were prisoned side by side. The orangutan
chattered with rage and his filthy snarling filled the chamber.
From Nita there was no sound. Wentworth did not turn his
head. He kept his eyes fixed upon the veil of the Mandarin and
still that cold small smile was on his lips.

"The answer will be no," he repeated and his voice was quiet
and decisive. For long moments the two men stared at each
other, stared despite that crimson veil that was between them,
stared while the bestial mouthings of the ape filled the room.
Then slowly the Mandarin straightened and Wentworth heard
once more the swish of weighted curtains. He felt suddenly
weak, felt moisture start in the palms of his hands, felt a bead of
sweat trickle coldly down his side. Ya Che's breath hissed out
between her teeth.

"I wish to be fair," the Mandarin said. "I do not believe you
fully realize the situation because of your injury. You shall have a
day to decide, but longer than that I will not be put off. Tomorrow at this hour, you shall give your answer...." He leaned
forward and his right hand flew out, the jade-guarded nail like
a knife point. "If it is *no,* you shall stand here as you do now, but
you shall face the wall and you shall see what goes on beyond
those bars. You shall watch it and afterwards you shall live to

remember. You will not ever be able to close your eyes. We shall make sure of that by removing the lids. Go!"

THE TWO giants spun Wentworth about, marched him across the room and more servants of the Mandarin took him in charge there with loaded guns against his spine, marched him back to the room where he had regained consciousness. Ya Che was thrust in with him and the door was shut. Wentworth heard heavy bars drop into place.

He stared about the room and saw that there were no windows. He felt the door and found it was solid steel. He felt beneath his arm and knew that the tool kit which might have got him from this hellish room was gone. He turned toward Ya Che. Her dead black eyes were upon his and there was a questioning on her usually expressionless face.

"No," she said, "there is no way out. I did not tell you before, but whatever fate you elect shall be mine also. The Mandarin has decreed it. And there is another thing that you should know.

"On New Year's eve, tomorrow, the Mandarin will strike in every resort of the city. Hotels and night clubs and cabarets, theaters and churches. Nothing shall escape. When the midnight whistles blow, he will kill tens of thousands and the next day doctors will find that they died of alcohol poisoning, or tobacco, or even coffee and tea. They are making the poison gases here even now.

"No man can avert that. Only a miracle…."

Wentworth's thoughts whirled with the fearful revelation. No man—she was right. No man imprisoned like this could avert the catastrophe. Better to accept the Mandarin's orders, save

Nita. After all, the Mandarin demanded only that a few men die. Suppose he killed them, eluded the men of the Mandarin who were sure to trail him. Might he not then succeed in staving off this disaster? Better that a few innocents should die than that ten thousand should perish.

Wentworth lifted his hands to his bandaged head, sagged across the room to his bed and fell upon it on his face. If he could get free—his driven thoughts ran—he might direct Boise into the proper activities to stop this catastrophe. Kirkpatrick, if he were free of whatever fearful thing held him in its grip and warped his mind, would know what to do automatically. His ingenious brain would work out that phase of it as well as Wentworth himself. But Kirkpatrick was out of his mind. Wentworth could find no other explanation of his criminal behavior in recent days, his refusal to take the obvious steps for the protection of the populace.

"The men the Mandarin wants you to kill," Ya Che was standing over him, speaking, "are Kirkpatrick, Boise, and the Mayor."

Wentworth thrust himself up from his bed, stared at her with widening eyes. Once more her face was expressionless; her black eyes deep pools of black light. But if he eliminated those men, then his freedom would do no good. Even to save his life and Nita's he would not break his pledged word. If he promised to kill those men, he would do it, and the city would tumble into destruction despite all he could do. Tens of thousands would die. He clenched his head wildly between squeezing palms.

Yes, there was a whisper in his brain, there was a way out. When he was marched forth tomorrow to face the Red Mandarin, he might smash his way out, leave Nita to her death... He sprang to his feet and his face was a mask of white suffering. That way, and that way only could he save those thousands of innocent lives!

"Kirkpatrick sent Nita into the Mandarin's trap, but it should not be held against him. He was under the power of the Mandarin, his soul was not his own."

Ya Che's voice was even-toned, expressionless. "Your Nita apparently detected that and wished to warn you. Kirkpatrick told her where you were and arranged the ambush."

Under the power of the Mandarin! Wentworth caught at that phrase of all that Ya Che had said. He had suspected that, whatever the words meant. He knew abruptly that his guess of the reason for Coslin's vision was true also. But all this pointed to Wu Chang. And Wu Chang was dead. His hands dropped from his head, hung upon his knees. This, too, would be the explanation of Steve Jardin's accusation of him, and of all those other false charges which the police had received. Those, all those, were under the power of the Mandarin—even as he and Nita were now. Good God! Was there no way out?

CHAPTER 17
DEATH IN THE SERAGLIE

WENTWORTH SAW that Ya Che watched him with a strange gleam in her dead black eyes. Her garb was Chinese no longer, but a robe of golden yellow that, cut low upon her magnificent breasts, clasped them closely and fell in heavy silken folds straight to her ankles. When she walked toward him, each limb was momentarily molded its entire length in the silken sheen. Her black hair swung upon her ivory shoulders.

"I was a servitor of the Red Mandarin," she said. "I freely confess that to you. I was his agent until he had my father slain, but now I am his foe. He knows that. I tell you this so that you may understand that what I say is the truth."

She came quite close and stood looking deeply into Wentworth's blue-gray eyes that now were like steel. The slow enigmatic smile spread upon her pale lips. "Now," she said slowly. "I am destined to become a slave girl, yours if you agree to what he wishes. If you refuse…" she shrugged. "He long has coveted me, and in his way, wooed me. Since my father is dead, there is no one left to protect me and to the victor belongs the spoils."

She came even closer so that her body almost touched his, so that once more the warm fragrance of her was about him like a cloud of scented forgetfulness.

"I would rather be thy slave, O man of steel," she said softly.

The smile was still on her lips and her ivory arms rose slowly until long slim hands rested on his shoulders. Her soft body touched his, and in itself, that was a caress. Her lids were heavy, but the black eyes beneath them still held his like a magnet.

"Tomorrow may bring death to us both," she whispered, "but tonight…."

"Tonight is yours," a harsh sibilant voice broke out in the room. "Use it well."

Ya Che whirled about, tense as a crouching cat. Wentworth's

eyes searched the shadows that lay in the corners of the room, but there was no one in the place save this woman with the warm fragrant body and himself.

"I have heard what you have told this man, Ya Che," came the voice and Wentworth knew that the Red Mandarin spoke, that he could see them. "By that, you have forfeited the right to live. Tomorrow you shall die, but tonight...."

The voice broke off and silence swept into the room, silence that their own tumultuous breathing could not break. Ya Che turned toward Wentworth again and the smile was upon her lips. There was recklessness and defiance in that smile, and there was promise. She came toward Wentworth slowly, hips swaying in a graceful walk, each limb molded in turn against the soft gleaming silk of her robe and Wentworth felt once more the gray clouds of hell swirl over his brain.

WITHIN FIFTEEN minutes, the men of the Red Mandarin would come for them, would come to demand the answer, to demand that Wentworth swear allegiance to him or watch Nita die horribly. Wentworth was ready. He was without a weapon. Nothing in the room would yield him one, unless the silken sheets of his bed would serve. Ya Che sat sullenly upon a lounge and smoke eddied upward from her pale lips. There was a heavy languor in all her movements. Abruptly she sat erect, flung her cigarette from her with a sharp irritability.

"What will you tell the Mandarin?" she asked.

Wentworth grinned. Strength was pulsing through his body. Since the moment he had repulsed Ya Che and laughed her out of his arms, the gray veil had withdrawn from his brain.

"You'll know shortly," he said lightly, "just practice patience, my dear."

The woman stood abruptly. "You are a fool!" she snapped. "I was insane to think you the man of steel you are supposed to be. Such a man I could have loved."

"I am sure of it," Wentworth murmured. "And you would have hypnotized him into loving you even as you hypnotized me into kow-towing before the Mandarin."

Ya Che started to her feet. "You are mad," she flung at him. "I did not hypnotize you."

"That's true, my dear," said Wentworth softly, "but you thought you did. I saw to that. I suspect you worked that little trick for the Mandarin or Kirkpatrick, on Coslin, on those clerks in the cigar stores who accused me."

"It was not I," Ya Che said vehemently. "It was Hsa Tze, who turned traitor in the end—the man you slew after he killed my father."

"Ah," said Wentworth softly. "Thanks."

The door opened abruptly and soft feet padded into the room.

"Come in," Wentworth called.

Two Chinese stood in the door with drawn automatics. They held their weapons close against their sides and ready. No sudden leap could reach them. Wentworth bowed suavely.

"Won't you have a cup of tea with me before we go?" he asked.

The Chinese looked at him impassively. One of them grunted an order to get out into the hall. Wentworth shrugged, made a wry face at Ya Che.

"I'm afraid they have no sense of humor," he said.

Wentworth's gun blazed again and the giant Nubian checked in

his charge, then came in, bellowing, sword poised!

Ya Che was frowning at him in puzzlement. "I do not under-stand you," she complained. "You must decide between killing your best friend and letting the woman you love be killed—and you laugh!"

Wentworth shrugged again, moving toward the hall; the Chinese close behind him with drawn guns, Ya Che beside him, Wentworth whistled a few bars of a blithe tune, stopped abruptly.

"Pshaw, I forgot my cigarettes," he said.

He turned and the two Chinese scowled at him, menacing him with the automatics.

"Go ahead," one ordered sharply.

Wentworth faced about again and as he did so, he swung out his right arm, swept Ya Che behind him and against one of the Chinese. The man cried out shrilly. Wentworth whirled with the stroke of his right arm and leaped upon the second Chinese, pinning his gun hand against his side. His fingers found a nerve center that paralyzed his grip and the automatic came free in his hand. He loosed the man and leaped past him, spinning the Chinese's body between himself and the other guard.

IN THE dim hall, his movements were like flickers of light. Not a full two seconds had elapsed since he had hurled Ya Che backward. She and the second Chinese had sprawled to the floor in an awkward tangle and the man was crying out shrilly, trying to get his gun hand clear. Wentworth slapped the second man with the automatic he had seized, stepped lightly to where Ya Che struggled and struck down. Then he yanked the woman to her feet.

"Quick, my darling," he said, "tell me the way to the laboratories."

The woman spat words at him, wrenched free of his hand. "I will not help you to free that Nita," she snarled. "You can find—"

Wentworth snapped up his fist and jarred her jaw. Ya Che slumped to the floor and he whirled away and ran back the direction the guards had brought him. He could hear a distant humming as though a stick had been poked into a hornet's nest. The Red Mandarin's hive was disturbed. The swarm of Chinese with steel stings would be upon him in short minutes of time. But there was a gay reckless smile upon Wentworth's lips. He had a fully loaded automatic in his hand. He was free for the moment and in the stronghold of the enemy. What more could the Spider ask?

Abruptly white light slashed like a sword across the corridor through which he raced. A wall curtain had whipped aside and through the opening three Chinese raced. Wentworth's gun spoke while his eyes—were still dazzled, but his hand had been long trained to the weight and swing of an automatic—his aim was almost an instinctive thing. He had caught the outline of the lead man in the race and it was enough. His lead flew true and the Chinese buckled with a shrill scream. A gun flew from his hand and whipped the silken curtains against the opposite wall, thudded softly to the floor. Twice more Wentworth fired and the other two men went down like clay pigeons on a target range.

A gay laugh whipped from Wentworth's lips.

He sprang forward and snatched up the gun that had fallen. He saw that the other two had been armed with knives and he thrust one beneath his belt. This was a fight in which he might well need every weapon he could get. But even in his haste, he paused beside the dead men to imprint upon their foreheads the seal of the Spider. Let these men know whom they battled. Let them see that not all their threatening arms could turn the Spider from his kill. Let them know fear.

He ducked through the opening from which the men had burst and let the curtains drop into place. He was in a small room. A low table stood in its middle with coins and cards spread upon it. These men had been playing at fan-tan when the alarm had come. But they must have been on guard, too. What was there to guard here?

WENTWORTH DUCKED behind the curtains that hid the walls of the room, as apparently they did everywhere in this domicile. He felt the walls with sensitive fingers. At last he found a section that seemed to yield slightly beneath his touch. He stiffened then, listening. Throughout the space about him, halls and connecting rooms, rang the shouts and cries of those who had found the bodies in the hall.

He pressed hard against the wall and it moved inward a distance of six inches then slid aside. He bounced through the opening and a Chinese with the huge bloated body of a eunuch whirled toward him, clutching a long-bladed sword. Behind him was a grill and through that he glimpsed the sense-drugging luxury of the seraglio where the Red Mandarin housed his concubines. Wentworth wanted no alarm of shots now. He whipped the knife from his belt, flung it with the same swift movement of his wrist. The eunuch cried out in fright, jerked his sword blade up. The glitter of light that was the knife streaked past it and sank its full depth in the man's gullet. The eunuch fell, coughing out his life.

In long strides, Wentworth crossed the guard room and peered through the grill work. Two young Chinese girls stood staring at him with fearful eyes. Their enameled faces could show little expression, but their eyes glittered. Suddenly one of them giggled, turned and ran. The other followed. Wentworth was on the point of whirling from them when he caught glimpse of a white face amid the luxurious shadows of silken hung walls—a face he recognized!

"Delia!" he cried. "Come here, Delia! It's Steve's friend."

Slowly the face came out of the shadows and Wentworth saw that it actually was the fiancée of Steve Jardin—the girl he had seen in the boy's tobacco shop on the night when first the horror of the Yellow Devil had struck the city—the girl Steve had accused him of kidnapping. She broke into a quick-legged run, reached the door and clung to the grill.

"Oh, thank God! Thank God!" she moaned. "I was afraid I would never escape. Is Steve with you?"

"I'm alone," Wentworth said, as the girl reeled backward with a little moan.

"WAIT," WENTWORTH cautioned grimly. He whirled to where the eunuch had fallen, snatched up the sword. With it, he smashed the lock of the door and Delia reeled out. She saw the body on the floor and shrank back, but Wentworth caught her hand and led her past it toward the door in the wall which had closed again.

"Listen, carefully," he told her. "In a few moments, I am going to cause a new alarm and the Chinese will follow me. When they do that, I want you to find your way out of here."

"I know the way out," Delia gasped. "I almost escaped once, but they caught me at the door."

"Good," Wentworth snapped grimly, "this time they will be too occupied with chasing me to find you. You get out of here and telephone this number..." he gave it to her swiftly. "My servant, Ram Singh, will answer. Give him this message. Kirkpatrick is under the power of drugs and hypnotism. The drugs have probably worn off now, but the hypnotism holds. Sometime tonight I will kill the person who holds him under his will. Ram Singh will know when that happens. He will then release Kirkpatrick and tell him that when the whistles blow the New Year out tonight, poison gas will be released in all theaters and hot spots—even in churches. Kirkpatrick must empty all those places, smash all liquor and liquid containers, seize all cigarettes. Got it?"

The girl repeated rapidly what Wentworth had said. "Good," he told her. "Now remember this. The lives of ten thousand persons depend on your getting out of here and 'phoning that message. Good-bye, and good luck!"

He tugged the door open. For a moment the girl's hands clung to his arm; then she released him. Gun in one hand, sword in the other, Wentworth slipped into the guard room. At the same instant, the curtains across the room parted and a Chinese entered. He saw Wentworth and a knife flew from his hand. Wentworth dropped to his knees. His sword arm circled once about his head and the blade swished forward. The man leaped backward but tangled in the curtain and the sword overtook him, sliced into his belly. He crumpled over the blade.

Wentworth darted to the hall, peered down its dark length.

"The way is clear," he called back softly. Delia, pale-faced, staggering a little from the carnage she had witnessed, went past him and slipped along the passageway like a wraith. Wentworth turned back to the corpse and took up the sword, wiped it clean. He went back to the entrance of the harem. There would be other entrances, he knew, and he must distract attention from Delia. He pulled open the door, strode swiftly across the big room and peered through an arch.

A dozen girls, some white, some Chinese, one Negress, were crouched fearfully there. He stepped toward them, making a horrible face. The girls screamed and Wentworth sprang among them whirling the sword above his head. They scattered like a flock of sparrows, shrieking. A door on the far side of the room flung open and another sword-armed eunuch stepped in. He spied Wentworth, set up a shrill shouting, retreated and swung the door shut.

Wentworth fled back the way he had come, skipped out into the hall past the bodies of the Chinese he had, slain and raced back to the room where he had been held prisoner with Ya Che. He made sure the locks could not be used, then hid inside. He was not a second too soon. He heard the whisper of many feet go past. He waited until there was silence; then he opened the door on emptiness. There was a tight smile upon his mouth as he sped then toward the crimson hall where the Mandarin sat upon his blood-colored throne. Nita was there in her steel sheathed cell, but that was not why Wentworth headed there. Nita would be safe until the Mandarin could hold Wentworth there to see her die—and Wentworth had no intention of being taken prisoner just yet.

IT TOOK five minutes to find the chamber where the Red Mandarin sat but Wentworth did not burst into the chamber. The Mandarin must die, but first there were other things that must be done. He listened behind, the black curtain.

"This is not treachery," Ya Che said vehemently. "I would like to see him torn limb from limb—after that woman has been killed. I tell you he demanded of me the way to the laboratories and that is where you will find him. He is the devil's own and he will find his way there." For moments then there was silence in the room. Presently the Mandarin spoke. "I believe you speak truth," his hissing voice stated. "We will go toward the laboratories. It is likely that this uproar in the harem was but intended to lead us astray."

Wentworth shrank aside behind the curtains. This was even better than he had hoped. He had made that demand of Ya Che, knowing that she would tell when she recovered consciousness what he had asked of her, planning to follow and find the laboratories. He had been afraid the delay with Delia would make him late for this rendezvous of which the Mandarin was unaware.

No movement within the room was audible and Wentworth parted the curtains a slight fraction of an inch to peer into that chamber of ebony and scarlet. The two guards were holding apart curtains directly opposite him, the giant Chinese and the giant Nubian, their long swords ready. The Mandarin wore a robe of imperial yellow.

"I think that we shall find our friend the Spider dead," the Mandarin mused. "There are too many traps along the way to the laboratories for those who do not know them."

"I hope he is not dead," said Ya Che. "I would not want him to die—too quickly."

There was the sibilant laughter of the Mandarin, then the curtains dropped behind them. In four long silent strides, Wentworth crossed the room and trailed. It was a long and torturous way they followed. Wentworth slipped from shadow to shadow in their wake. Twice the giant Nubian stalked back along the passage while the group waited, stalked back with that giant sword tensely ready for a murderous stroke. Once Wentworth shrank behind a curtain and held his breath while his own sword was poised on a guard. Once Wentworth retreated before his advance and was nearly trapped when his brushing hand let out a thread of light from a side chamber. Luckily, at that instant, the Negro turned back and Wentworth escaped detection. Finally— the musty odors that thronged the corridor told Wentworth they were far underground—the man and woman and the two giant guards went through a door where hooded lights glittered on chemists' flasks and tubes.

Outside, Wentworth paused. This was his goal. If he could destroy what lay behind this door, kill the Red Mandarin who held Kirkpatrick under his domination; if Delia could meantime reach a telephone and give his message to Ram Singh, then he might triumph in his battle with these forces of murder and destruction. So many ifs—the odds were fearful. But not until these things had been accomplished might he think of Nita and go to her rescue and save her from the horror and death that threatened.

Behind those doors, he knew the Red Mandarin contrived some new mortal trap, for him. All along the way to this underground fastness he had repeatedly manipulated small hidden levers that prevented alien intrusion. He had voiced his doubts that even the Spider could have slipped through unharmed, yet fear and doubt drove him on. Wentworth felt the weight of the sword in his hand, the comfortable pressure of the automatic thrust beneath his belt, the other that lay in his palm.

Behind this door the odds would be at least three to one, even if the men who worked there did not join in the battle. But three bullets were soon sped, and a sword in his hands was as mighty as those the giants wielded. Wentworth's lips curved in a thin smile. If he retreated along this hall, those same traps that had been turned aside before might snare him. If he waited here, he would he trapped in narrow halls where there was no room to fight off death.

There was only one thing to do. Wentworth found the latch of the door, eased it up with the tip of the sword. He flung the door wide and leaped into the laboratory!

CHAPTER 18
THE SPIDER STRIKES

A ROUND THE walls of the laboratory, benches were piled high with chemicals and glassware. A cauldron bubbled beneath a tin chimney that sucked off swirling greenish fumes. Over these, a dozen men were busy while one with a thick pad of papers in his hand walked behind them and supervised the work. In the middle of the room, the Red Mandarin stood, Ya Che at his side. Behind him were poised the two guards with their naked swords.

Wentworth flung his flat mocking laughter into the fume-heavy room, the sinister mirth of the Spider.

"The Spider is here!" he cried. "He brings death!"

The automatic in his left hand punctuated the sentence and the man with the thick wad of papers in his fist lurched face down on the floor. The two giant guards whirled, faces twisted hideously by battle rage. Their swords flashed up and like one man they sprang toward Wentworth. He had a glimpse of the Red Mandarin spinning about, of a slender-nosed gun that sprang to his hand.

Then he leaped aside from the attack of the two guards so that the Nubian's attack was blocked by that of his companion—so that both bodies shielded him from the Mandarin's gun. The giant Chinese was upon him instantly. He had flung the sword high above his head, slicing downward. The edge of that blade would cut Wentworth in half as cleanly as if his body

193

were so much hot butter. Wentworth's sword flicked forward faster than powder-sped lead. He made no attempt to parry the blow, but sent the curved edge of the scimitar whistling at the giant's middle.

Fright twisted the man's face. He flinched backward, checking the sweep of his blade, but he was too late. The razor edge flicked across his belly and the flesh opened like the lips of a hideous mouth. He screamed then in fear, not with pain, for he had felt none as yet, felt nothing but the numbness of the shock. He knew the damage that those razor edges could do. He staggered back, sword dropping, hands clasping his belly. Wentworth's gun blazed again and the giant Nubian checked in his charge, then came in, bellowing, sword poised. Wentworth saw blood fleck out on his ribs where the bullet had gone in, saw the Chinese giant crumble with red streaming between his belly-clenching fingers. He wasted no more bullets on the Negro. His sword flew up to meet the sweep of the other's blade and the clash of steel rang like a temple gong through the room.

Quick as light, the Negro's sword disengaged, swept in a sideways stroke. Wentworth's teeth bared in a tight grin of hate. A side stroke has the advantage if the opponent does not know how to meet it, but against an experienced fighter it means death for the user. This Negro, if he thought at all, did not reckon that Wentworth knew how to handle so barbaric a weapon as this curved, heavy sword. He swept it in a savage, sideways gouge for Wentworth's throat.

Wentworth sprang back two full feet, swayed forward again instantly. In that moment, the blade had whined past his chest.

The giant Negro's arm followed his blade, his body twisted slightly with the violence of his stroke. His right flank was wide open, without protection until he could check his heavy blade and reverse its swing.

Wentworth's blade was still high above his head where it had countered the sweep of the Nubian's sword. As he swayed forward again, he cut downward with the sure saberman's drag that makes the edge bite home. It bit. The Nubian's head fell over on his left shoulder, fastened only by a thread of flesh. Wentworth hurled past him, eyes flashing about the room.

THE RED MANDARIN and Ya Che had vanished! Only two Chinese were left in the room. They were dragging the body of the first man Wentworth had shot toward a narrow door that gaped beneath a chemist's bench. Wentworth's gun blazed twice as he leaped forward and the two men dropped. The door snapped shut and Wentworth, crouching with ready automatic in the middle of the shop, was like a thwarted panther, beaten from his kill. His lips twisted back from his teeth and red rage gleamed in his eyes.

It was only for an instant. He dropped his sword and hurled himself upon the tangled bodies of the three Chinese. He wrenched that of the supervisor over on his back and with a cry of triumph, seized the wad of papers from his hand. It took only a glance to tell Wentworth that his first guess as to the character of the papers was right. They contained the formulas of the poison gases that were being brewed here for the destruction of the people!

Clenching them in one hand, Wentworth sprang toward the

benches. His sword smashed. Glass tinkled on the floor, crucibles and bottles of white and brown and green powder broke in a thousand fragments beneath his flail of steel.

Fumes burned upward from the porcelain where the mess was stirred—brown fumes and white fumes like smoke. It took a minute of furious work to clear those shelves of all materials, then Wentworth sprang toward the door. Once, on the way, he paused, stooped over the body of the giant he had slain, then he wrenched the door open.

He turned, emptied his automatic into the room, not wildly, but deliberately. His first shot pierced the base of the great boiling crucible beneath the chimney. The rest of his bullets smashed into gas storage vats stacked against one wall. Then he slammed the door and fled. His keen eyes flashed ahead of him and his memory ticked off the traps that the Red Mandarin had avoided. Above him, he heard the clash of great brazen gongs the shouts and shrill imprecations of the aroused servitors of the Red Mandarin.

If the place had been a hornet's nest over his escape, it became now a den of tigers. Howls of rage flung down the corridors. The pad-pad of running feet was like the marching of an army. Finally Wentworth reached the goal toward which he raced, a right angle turn in the narrow hallway where one man might stand off a dozen—as long as his ammunition lasted. Wentworth was berserk with killing rage now. He had destroyed gas and seized the formulas, but it was probable that the supplies for this night's ten thousand murders already had gone to the appointed places. He would prevent further murders, but for tonight, if he would save those who, gaily celebrating the death of an old year, might be drinking their own doom in a glass of champagne, he must still battle on. He must wipe out this Red Mandarin whose mind held Kirkpatrick's brain in leash.

A horde of Chinese poured along the halt. Wentworth laid his sword beside him and his two automatics spat streams of fiery death. For a full minute, he held the rush in check, blocking their path with the corpses of their fellows, then the charge came on. With a roar of defiance, Wentworth sprang to his feet, hurled the empty guns in their faces. He snatched up the sword and whirled it over his head and down.

It struck a Chinese upon the crown of his head and bit through. The man's face fell in halves. Wentworth wrenched the sword free, bracing his foot against the man's chest. Then he struck again, again, again....

On his third blow, the sword ate into the joint of a man's shoulder where it swelled into his neck and the steel wedged tight. There was no time to wrench and tug. The charge was upon him. A curse between his teeth, Wentworth caught up man and sword and hurled them into the press.

IT WAS a valiant fight, one man against a dozen, but it could not go on forever. Already blows had reached past his guard and his arms were numb with their assault. He had no weapons except his fists. He hurled himself upon the Chinese, striking with bone-crunching strength, but in the end he went down, smothered with numbers.

His flesh crawled, waiting for the death thrust of a knife, but strangely it did not come. His arms were yanked behind him and bound. He was jerked to his feet and a dozen hands gripped him as he was marched, stumbling and reeling, along the corridor of death. He saw then what havoc he had wrought—saw dead men lying in contorted stiffness upon the floor—saw the spitting hate in the faces about him. He threw back his head and laughed. It was flat and mocking and horrible and the men who held him captive shrank from him even while they held him with trembling hands. He was still chuckling terribly when they thrust him into the room where the Red Mandarin sat upon his bloody throne….

The man's rage was apparent in every inch of his rigid body, in the long nailed hands that clutched tensely upon the blood-colored arms of the throne.

"Down," he shrieked. "Put the son of a pig and turtle upon his knees."

A half dozen hands wrenched at him. Anger flooded Wentworth's veins with strength. He whipped his shoulders clear and strode to the foot of the throne with his arms bound behind him.

"Kneel to you, O unclean one?" he snarled. He threw back his head and laughed again. The chill menace of it made the men who rushed upon him shrink back, even in the face of the Red Mandarin's rage. "Kneel to you? Not while I live, you bowl of filth! And it would be wise, if you did not kill me."

The Red Mandarin held an automatic in his right hand now, leveled at Wentworth's breast. He held it in a hand that trembled, but Wentworth did not believe it was fear.

"If you want the formula for your gases," Wentworth said, more calmly, "it would be wise if you did not kill me."

The Mandarin sank back upon his throne, and his voice rose in shrill Chinese. Silence dropped, upon the assembly, upon the men who had seized Wentworth. Finally one answered in a quavering voice. The Mandarin screamed with rage. The gun in his hand spat and a man shrieked out his life before its muffled echoes had died.

"You will tell me where these formulas are," said the Red Mandarin, his voice hissing.

Wentworth shook his head and a mirthless smile craved his lips. "Not if you boiled me in oil, louse," he said quietly. "There is just one way you can get those formulas back and that is by turning me and Miss van Sloan free. If you will do that, I will tell you on my pledged word the location of the formulas. I swear to you—the Spider swears to you—that those formulas are not destroyed, but hidden."

THE MANDARIN chattered again and men raced away to do his bidding. Wentworth guessed that he had ordered a search for the formulas. Behind the scarlet throne, the curtains swirled aside and Ya Che came into the room. Her face was twisted with hate and before her she thrust Delia, her slave girl's costume half torn from her, her faced bruised and bleeding.

"I caught this one near the entrance," said Ya Che. "The Spider set her free!"

Wentworth's lips still smiled, but his heart sank down within him and his stomach became a stone. If Delia had failed to escape then Ram Singh had received no warning—death would still stride the streets tonight. Good God! He had a desperate battle to fight before, but now it became stupendous. Not only must he escape, but he must flee at once if he were to stave off the destruction of tens of thousands of lives.

The Red Mandarin had not turned toward Ya Che. He stared at Wentworth and for the first time this night, the sound that came from beneath the crimson veil was not rage, but mirth.

"Excellent, Ya Che," he said. "I think you have blocked a little plan of my friend, the Spider. A little plan to warn of the executions that come tonight, that come—" Strangely, he pulled up his sleeve and glanced at an American wrist watch "come within the hour."

His sibilant, hissing laughter filled the curtained room.

"Spider, you have one chance," he said. "Tell me where you hid the formulas and I will give you the same chance you had before; the choice of killing those men who must be removed and becoming wealthy beyond your dreams… or of seeing the spectacle I promised you."

A stir at the back of the room heralded the return of the men the Mandarin had sent away. He questioned them in clattering Chinese and the answer he received dropped silence once more upon the room.

"You seem to have done a very complete job in the laboratory, Spider," said the Red Mandarin. "My men had to wear gas masks to search it. Perhaps the papers are somewhere about you?"

Wentworth laughed. "No, they are not on me, swine. Nor will you ever find them unless I tell you their whereabouts. And you cannot torture me into revealing where they are."

For moments of silence, the blank veiled face regarded him. Slowly the head nodded. "I believe you tell the truth. I do not believe even my little pleasant rites, such as the Seven Heavens of Indescribable Happiness would wrest it from you. But there is another way…."

Ya Che had advanced to his side, having thrust Delia into the hands of two men, and a cruel smile twisted her lips. "Yes," she whispered, "there is always—*the mating of the orangutan!*"

CHAPTER 19
THE SPIDER'S PREY

WENTWORTH FOUGHT to keep his lips smiling, but his face went stiff with fear. The Red Mandarin laughed with a silken swish, the curtains went up.

"Yes, yes," he said, "there is always the mating. Ya Che, you are full of ideas. I must give you credit for most of my accomplishments."

Resolutely, Wentworth kept his eyes on the Mandarin. "I swear to you," he said slowly, "that if you do this thing, you shall never have the formulas. I swear that you shall die if I have to return from ten thousand hells to kill you."

The Mandarin chuckled. "Your mind is strong, Wentworth," he said. "I think you might resist torture. But you have a big heart. I wonder if your resolution would not weaken if I offered you a pistol with one bullet, one bullet with which to halt the mating—once it has begun."

His voice crackled in Chinese and men seized Wentworth, twisted him about so that he faced the cells against the wall. The orangutan was close against the wall nearest Nita's cell. He had thrust a red-haired arm out between the bars of his cell into hers and he was fighting with little growls of rage and thwarted fury to wriggle his great body after that arm. Nita was crouched against the far wall of her cell, her face white and rigid with fright, her eyes staring at that fearful hairy arm. She turned her head, saw Wentworth a prisoner, saw the crowd of men that held him, and she smiled piteously. Her chin came up and she stood erect and brave. Her clothing was the same and the lines of her body, revealed more than hidden by that deliberately alluring garb, were exquisite.

"A tender morsel, eh, Spider?" chuckled the Mandarin. "Now you or I…."

Wentworth's voice was tight with fury. "I have warned you," he grated out. "If she is harmed, your formulas will be lost to you forever."

"Free his right hand only," said the Mandarin softly. "Then take this revolver and place it half way to the cage."

These things were swiftly done, but four men held on to his freed arm, held him with all their weight and strength.

"Now, Wentworth," said the Mandarin. "We will forget the violence that has past. You are about to see this wonderful spectacle. You have only to reveal the hiding-place of the formulas— promise to do what I have asked and you will be freed. Your Nita will be freed. Continue to refuse, and your Nita dies a very horrible death only a woman could contrive." He raised his hand and in the wall between the two cells, a small door lifted an inch.

"If you wish to stop that door from rising, you have only to say 'I promise,' Wentworth, and you will be allowed to have the gun and kill the orangutan. But I would not wait too long. The shock might be too much for dear Nita."

The door raised another inch. Abruptly, the orangutan seemed to sense what was happening. He sprang from the bars to the openings in one great bound and clutched at the bottom of the rising door, straining at it. His bellow was thunderous. The Mandarin chuckled.

"The challenge of the bull orangutan," he said. "A pleasant sound, eh?"

Despite her courage, Nita was shrinking back against the far wall of her cell again. But not one word of petition, not one word to Dick did she say. She knew the battle that he fought, knew that the cause was just. Wentworth surged helplessly against the hands that held him. His eyes started from his head. Sweat bathed his forehead.

"You can't do this! You can't!" he said hoarsely.

THE DOOR had slid another two inches. The beast fought it with terrible strength. He bent forward and thrust his bestial face to the crack, saw Nita. Slavering foam fell from his lips. His roars were increasing now.

Wentworth stood rigidly. He had ceased to strain against the arms that held him. Dear God, were all the lives in the world worth the suffering that would be Nita's? It was a cry from his heart, but his mind sat in cold judgment. He was the cause of this, he alone. If his love had not touched Nita, this horror would not now face her. He twisted his head toward the Red Mandarin.

"In heaven's name," he said, "don't do this thing. I have

millions I will give you. I will be your slave, anything, anything, but spare her this."

The Red Mandarin leaned forward. "Do you promise?" he demanded.

Wentworth's heart cried that he did. His mind twisted tight the thumbscrews of torture. He could not yield. If he saved Nita, thousands would die.

"Damn you!" howled Wentworth, "can't you understand. If you do this to her, you will never get the formulas, not if you cut me to pieces by tiny bits. I will not talk."

The door slid up a foot and with a scream, the orangutan wrenched it from its socket, crawled through into Nita's cell. She stood rigid and unmoving against the wall, her eyes set on the beast's. The orangutan, now that he was within the cell, stood motionless for a moment. A small whimpering rose in its throat. Its shaggy head sagged forward and it shuffled toward Nita. She shrieked once and slumped to the floor in a dead faint.

Wentworth wrenched violently at the hands that held him, but even his fury-driven strength was no match for their numbers. They swayed forward a foot, reeled back. But they held. The orangutan was squatted beside Nita now. Making queer soft noises in this throat, the beast reached out and plucked at her clothing. The filmy silk ripped loose in his hand.

The Mandarin chuckled. "Not much protection in silk," he murmured. "I think the mating will soon begin, Wentworth. Do you promise?"

The orangutan ripped the last shred of clothing from Nita, slid a red-furred arm beneath her and twisted its bestial face toward the men who stared in upon him. He bared his teeth in a snarl. Wentworth stiffened in the grip of the men who held him. His teeth were bare, too… Suddenly he threw back his head and from his chest and throat burst a savage screaming roar. It filled the room, banged against the padded walls. Nita stirred in the embrace of the beast and Wentworth screamed again, and the sound that came from him was the mating challenge of the orangutan!

The orang sprang to the back of the cell, Nita across his arm, found that he was blocked with solid walls. He threw Nita upon the floor and whirled, baring his teeth. Wentworth screamed again and an answering roar came from the ape. Wentworth felt the holds upon his arms trembling. He bellowed out the challenge again. Abruptly the orang flung at the bars. He was chattering with rage. He shook the steel slats until they trembled. He wrenched at them savagely. Wentworth screamed again, then he jerked free of the clasp upon his arms, hurled himself toward the revolver that lay upon the floor. He knew that in the next moment he might die beneath the knives and bullets of the Chinese behind him, but if he could snatch up that revolver and fire one shot. Nita at least would be safe from this fiendish torture that the Mandarin planned.

THE ORANGUTAN put another meaning on Wentworth's wild charge. He thought it was the attack of a male that challenged his ownership of this queer female within the cage. With a screaming that battered into insignificance every other sound, the orang wrenched at the bars again, bent them, and bounded out into the room, wicked small eyes set upon Wentworth. He beat upon his chest with drumming fists, bared the yellow fangs.

Wentworth was still two yards from the revolver, which was almost between the orang's feet. Without a moment's pause in movement, he spun to his right, dived bodily among the Chinese who were rushing to meet him. They had frozen in their tracks, terrified by the phenomenal strength of the orangutan and now they turned in pell-mell flight. The orang sprang among them, pursuing that male who had challenged him. He tossed Chinese right and left. Their knives were nothing to him. They pecked at the sinews of his arms but bothered him no more than the sting of fleas.

Wentworth crawled through the mêlée toward the Red Throne. Ya Che was fleeing through the parted curtains, the Red Mandarin behind her. Wentworth mounted the steps in a rush, dived for the legs of the Mandarin and brought him crashing down. The curtains swung shut behind Ya Che, but Wentworth at last had closed with the monster who had struck at the heart of the nation. He locked his hands about the man's neck, but was compelled to loose it to strike aside the knife thrust of the Chinese. He reeled up from the man's prostrate figure, staggered back and his shoulders brought up hard against the throne.

The Red Mandarin sprang to his feet and a snarl hissed out from beneath his crimson veil. A gun flashed in his hand from the voluminous sleeve of his yellow robe. Even as it spat flame and lead, Wentworth hurled forward. A shocking stab of pain numbed his chest, but he plunged on. His hands closed upon the automatic and he wrenched violently. Bones cracked dully in the Mandarin's hand. He screamed and his jade nail guards dug at Wentworth's throat.

Wentworth's fist flew out, smashed the Mandarin back against the wall. The captured revolver convulsed in his fist, belching out lead at point-blank range. The Mandarin screamed again, screamed in an agony that human flesh could not support. He clawed at the silken curtains. His yellow robe was spotted with crimson, polka-dotted with gouts of blood. Wentworth became aware that the automatic in his hand no longer spewed lead, that he was straining at a trigger that no longer released death. But no more bullets were needed.

A scream that changed into a sobbing breath bubbled from the Mandarin. The red foam of death dribbled from beneath the crimson mask and he crumpled slowly to the dais, his hands tearing the silken curtains. They ripped loose from their fastenings, bellied in a black cloud from the wall and collapsed about the fallen Mandarin in a silken shroud, a black shroud that settled with a rustling whisper that was like hissing laughter.

Wentworth felt, more than heard, the horrid laughter that tore from his own throat. He had killed the Red Mandarin, had saved Nita from the grasp of the orangutan, but out in the city tens of thousands would go to their death within the hour unless he could give the warning. Delia Hardesty had been trapped, had been unable to reach a phone and give Ram Singh the warning that would have meant salvation.

He must escape this building and give the warning. The gun dropped from his hand. He pressed both fists, to his chest and felt the welling of blood from the wound in his chest. He looked down at it curiously, and a bitter smile twisted his lips. Life was seeping out through that hole where Mandarin's bullet had ploughed. Sluggishly he turned his head toward the room.

THE ORANG still fought among the Chinese. He held one man's body by the head and struck with his fists as if that body were a mere rag. Wentworth peered toward the cells. Delia had joined Nita there and together they had crawled through the small door between the cages. They were huddled there now, and Nita clutched in her hand the revolver which contained one bullet. Delia shouldn't be there. She should be 'phoning the warning.

Slowly, Wentworth staggered toward the twisted bars. He fell twice in his slow progress across the room. There was no living soul save himself now in the main room, himself and the orang. Wentworth fell again and lay still for a long moment. Finally he thrust himself up on stiff arms and stared once more at the orang. The beast was not looking at him, but toward the spot where the Red Mandarin had torn down the silken curtain. There was an archway there and across a narrow room, Ya Che was beating her fists upon a closed door.

With a small whimpering cry, the orang bounded to the throne, Ya Che heard him, twisted her head about and screamed. Abruptly the door came open under her hand and she hurled through it. The orang went through behind her. Wentworth reeled to his feet, fought his slow way back toward the throne. Suddenly room and bodies of the dead whirled about him. Darkness cut out the scene.

WHEN HE recovered consciousness, he heard clipped familiar accents, a voice he knew with a ring in it he had not heard in long days, the voice of Stanley Kirkpatrick. Wentworth fought his way up through yards of black silk that, seemed to shroud his eyes. He opened them finally and found Kirkpatrick glaring down at him angrily.

"We stopped all the parties in town" he snapped at Wentworth. "And we tested the drinks on dogs. It killed them. For that reason I'm going to forgive you for kidnapping me, but the next time…" Wentworth grinned wryly, twisted his head and found Nita was crouched beside. She wore Kirkpatrick's overcoat.

Delia was beside her. She bent forward.

"They didn't catch me until after I had telephoned the message," she said swiftly. "I couldn't tell you that for fear they would know. Mr. Kirkpatrick traced the call and found us here. All the Chinese are arrested."

Nita dropped on her knees, her hands touched his face and they were cool. "Don't worry about your wound, darling," she said softly. "The doctor says it just missed your right lung, but that you'll pull through all right."

The words thudded at Wentworth's brain. He felt comfortable where he lay. Too comfortable to talk. But something was stirring in his brain, a something that should come out. Suddenly he remembered. The orangutan!

"The orangutan!" he gasped out. "What happened to it?"

Nita's face went stiff with fear. "We can't find him anywhere. We can't find the woman, Ya Che," she said in a choked voice. "They've hunted everywhere."

"We'll find them," Kirkpatrick broke in. "There are several things I want to ask Dick if the doctor says it's okay."

Wentworth heard the murmur of the doctor's voice and Kirkpatrick promising he would be brief. "Where are the formulas hidden?" he asked. "We want to find and seize them."

Wentworth frowned. "I put them… in the stomach… of the dead Mongol in the laboratory."

"In the stomach?"

WENTWORTH NODDED. "I killed him with a stomach-cut, and shoved the papers in there. I had hidden them, but even if the Chinese had found them, they would be no good. Blood would have hidden all the writing, pulped the paper."

"Not so clever, these Chinese," Kirkpatrick grinned. "Now, tell me if you knew who the Red Mandarin was. We know now because we've lifted the crimson veil, but you haven't seen the man's face yet."

A hypodermic the doctor had given him strengthened Wentworth. He smiled at Nita. "All the evidence pointed to just one man," he said slowly. "I'm not dead sure of all the details of it just now, but I've already given you fragments of the whole plot. The man indicated was Wu Chang. For a while, his apparent murder fooled me, but Ya Che recovered far too quickly from the supposed death of her beloved father. She was quite unfilial about it. I began to suspect that it was all just a trick to confuse me because I had come too close to the truth.

"Furthermore, there was the Denict Cigarette Company—it was a perfect setup. And there had to be some kind of tie-up. There were a number of possible ramifications. While ordinary tobacco meant death to the smokers, the Denict Company could coin money. When the other companies had been forced out of business, the manufacturers of Denict cigarettes could start doping the nation that way—slowly, of course—but with in a few months, he could have made drug addicts of the whole populace.

"In addition to this, wholesale murders would so unnerve the organization of the government that the man behind them could capture any prize he coveted. That man, provided he were clever enough, and ruthless enough, could hold America in the palm of his hand. And that man—the Red Mandarin—could have been but one person—Wu Chang!"

"You're right," Kirkpatrick conceded grimly. "Next time you tell me anything, I'll believe you, Dick. It might interest you to know that none of the witnesses who accused you of being tied up with the tobacco deaths accuses you any longer. I found that out from Boise while we were racing down here. They began to retract on Christmas Eve."

"Naturally," Wentworth whispered. "They were hypnotized. The man who held them under his will died Christmas Eve, and the spell was broken."

His eyes closed wearily, then snapped open in sharp alarm. A horrible cry rang through the corridors, but it was dim in the distance. It was the scream of a woman terribly injured— terribly afraid. It rose high and clear through the night—three, four times. Even in its agony, it was plainly recognizable as Ya Che's voice.

"The roof!" Kirkpatrick barked. "The roof, quickly!"

He plunged from the room and long minutes afterward there continued a fusillade that echoed through the night. Kirkpatrick came back into the room heavily; every eye centered on him as he stopped just inside the doorway. He shuddered uncontrollably.

"We were too late," he said. "Ya Che was dead. The orangutan had mated."